Che and the Calaway Girls

Nora Seton

Regal House Publishing

Published by
Regal House Publishing, LLC
Raleigh, NC 27612
All rights reserved

ISBN -13 (paperback): 9781646030712
ISBN -13 (epub): 9781646030965
Library of Congress Control Number: 2020941110

Interior and cover design by Lafayette & Greene
lafayetteandgreene.com
Cover images © by Patinya_P_ang/Shutterstock

Regal House Publishing, LLC
https://regalhousepublishing.com

Printed in the United States of America

For Hugh and Madeleine

MONDAY

1

There are no Baptists in this dream. It's a party and all the guests are dancing. People drink Bloody Marys from tall iced-tea glasses. Their celery leaves flutter as the first winds of a storm push through the open windows. My neighbors have gathered under a chandelier and I join them.

Here's Julia. Did you design that dress, Julia? Is blue the new black?

Oil is going to hit sixty dollars a barrel, Julia. You need to go long on oil.

Where is your ex now, Julia? Men can't hit their wives anymore—did you hear?

Not even the Saudis want eighty-dollar oil. It's unsustainable.

What should we wear for the hurricane, Julia? Have you designed a trench coat? All the designers put out trench coats.

I've named a new rose for my dogs, Julia. It's a florabunda.

By God, that's a mint leaf in my drink.

Suddenly I hear my mother's voice. *Your grandma Bisskit used to mix yellow dye into our margarine, so that no one would know we were sharecroppers.*

Mother? I say. *Mother?* I look everywhere. I push through dancing bodies to find her. I look behind a sofa. The party noise is deafening. Finally I see a door. Hanging on it is a porcelain cross with Jesus—sad, kind of accusatory, impaled by three nails. I know my mother is behind that door. She promised us the four-nailers were infidels.

I'm going to open that door.

Don't open that door! I wish someone would say to me, and reach with gentle fingers into my dream and pluck me out.

I open the door.

And—*boom!*—my mother flies out at me like a poltergeist, screaming fit to pierce my ears, *Let me go!*

1

Normally I'm a great obeyer, a born minion, but this is a dream and I'm sure she's forgotten to tell me something that will rock my world. I race after her. Suddenly we're in the driveway. The wind is blowing hard now. My mother is loading up the family station wagon with all her belongings. She sucks the last whisper of nicotine from a cigarette and shoves a heaped hamper of clothing into the cargo space. My mother grew up in South Carolina and never signed on for what she called the "Latino model" of hurricanes—the no-power, no-plumbing, no-cold-beer variety. I'm having a conniption—a river of tears.

She turns to me from where she is (cinching her mattress to the car roof) and shrieks.

Let me go!

And I wake up. In the dark. My heart in my mouth.

I have this dream before every hurricane. There's a television station in my brain that airs this horrible rerun when low pressure swirls toward the Gulf. I wake up drenched in sweat and trembling. I pry open the petals of my unconscious like a compliant schoolgirl, but I can't understand what it means.

Let me go?

But I'm not holding on. I don't want my mother here. She did enough damage while she was alive, kicking at life and leaving a legacy of bruised souls.

My mother hated Houston. She said it was the bottom of the pickle barrel when it came to single-family insane asylums. Or maybe just one pickle above her childhood in the tobacco-farming Pee Dee of South Carolina. There, my mother and her sister, Loretta, stuffed their belongings into their pillowcases every few months as their parents traded one crumbling sharecropper's cottage for another, each one with dripping sinks, peeling Formica, and grim-faced neighbor children who stared from rotting porches. The family moved relentlessly in the wake of Grandpa Richter, whose skin, hair, teeth, and toenails were pure tobacco brown. My mother said she always reckoned his insides were brown, too, until the day he fell off the curing barn and proved his blood was still red. Bright red, my mother said.

My mother didn't so much grow up as quit childhood. The color brown, linked forever to dried tobacco leaves, became for her a Biblical abomination. She fed her three daughters white foods. She dressed us in cotton bleached to the color of coconut meat. And she, who as a child had been frog-marched through schools in church castoffs, decorated our school uniforms to hide their cheapness. She basted ribbons onto hems and swapped out plastic discs for mother-of-pearl buttons that shimmered like big dewdrops.

What was my mother wearing in my dream? Her pink shirtdress? A pale blue shift? But I can't find it, the dream data, and I have the feeling that I had it and misplaced it, as though I once touched air and am doomed to try to again for the rest of my life.

5:10 a.m. Through the shutters, the streetlights cast a muted glow. Years back the mayor reduced city wattage to save money, after oil prices went to the moon. Then crude tanked, but the streetlights stayed dim.

Drifting back to sleep will be someone else's story. I flick on the radio and listen to the morning's fishing report.

I used to fish when I was in high school, when Clyde Holcombe or Justin Domaine would let me come with them to Galveston. We waded into the sticky surf and scrambled out along the rock jetties, our feet grabbing on to the slippery granite as though we had ten talons for toes.

My mother told me once, apropos of nothing, that she was "okay" if I married Justin Domaine. No matter that he was born in Corpus to a shrimping family and mowed lawns after school. No matter that he was gay, lower on the social ladder than any minorities of the time, and that he died in a car wreck my senior year of high school. My mother continued to cough him up as a potential mate, long after he had passed, sometimes remembering to ask if he'd had a brother

cut of the same cloth. She put forward the simple men, because her father had always invented some pied story for why
the family had to up and move, time after time roping their
belongings onto the roof of the Rambler until its suspension
sagged and its muffler raked the road. Fishermen, my mother said, picked a patch of water and stayed put.

This morning, a radio call-in from Perdido Pass claims
he's using three-inch croakers to catch speckled trout.

"You can go larger on the croakers," he says. "Especially
before a hurricane. Give the fish something else to think
about. Distract 'em."

The next thing I know, my telephone is ringing.

"Texas? Hey, Texas! You awake?"

I recognize the nicotine-shredded voice of Leona Milana.
Lung cancer is a lousy way to go. That's what her doctor
said. So Leona gave up cigarettes two years ago and took up
obesity.

"I'm awake," I say.

"Julia, we got an emergency here," Leona says. "We've
been hacked."

I work as a designer for Pitti Palazzo, one of the Italian fashion houses that rubs shoulders with Burberry and
Chanel. Leona Milana is the office manager of Pitti's studio
in New York City. Her voice this morning has a peculiarly
wide sound, like maybe she gained another two hundred
pounds. I love Leona, but they'll have to haul her out of the
Garment District in a crane sling one day.

"What did they take?" I say.

"They didn't take anything. They saw everything. We need
new. Wait, here's Marty."

Pitti Palazzo's celebrity designer for ten gold-mine years
has been Marty K. (he left the Katzenburg in Scarsdale). M.K.
was the man behind the platform Mary Jane, the revival of
turquoise and brown, the super-skinny capri with the swinging baby-doll minidress look—and I was the woman behind

him. He changed his sex a few years ago, which meant he had the opportunity to name both a men's cologne ("MK" 2009) and a woman's perfume ("Mia" 2016).

The "I'm a virgin again!" campaign was not my idea. M.K. picks up the phone. "I'm going to be a mom, Julia! We can launch a children's line!"

M.K. is the reason few people have ever heard my name. He takes my designs, altering them only to shorten a sleeve by one-eighth of an inch, or enlarge a button, before consenting to have the famous MK appliqué sewn on. For this MK in gold thread, superstars across the globe whip out their credit cards before the last runway model has snorted her celebratory cocaine. "I'm the show, baby," M.K. likes to remind me.

Now M.K. makes an exasperated noise. "Julia, some golem hacked into my 2021 resort collection. Probably a Russian. They'll be making my designs in Shanghai before lunch. What do you have down there? What do you have on your walls?"

I hear Leona in the background. "Tell her to send up some of those tamales. She doesn't hafta wait till Christmas."

M.K. says, "Julia, I need you to send me JPEGs of everything you have."

M.K. gives the phone back to Leona. "It's a disaster up here," Leona says. "The Italians are all *aiuto aiuto!* M.K.'s mother won't come to the ultrasounds. I know you got a hurricane coming, but this is an emergency."

I pull a sweatshirt over my nightgown, tie back my hair, and tiptoe up to the attic. To my studio. One switch and half a dozen daylight fluorescents flame brightness into the room.

Good morning, girls.

Life-size female figures make a frieze across my walls. They are drawn in oil stick, smudged, wiped, painted, patched with swatches of fabric, and itemized by color names. Wispy, walking breezily off the plaster in skirts, dresses, trousers, long-sleeved and short-sleeved blouses—they are my silent army, like Emperor Qin's terra-cotta soldiers.

This crop of drawings was slated for winter 2022. I used silk velvet and turned it into coats over silk-and-wool sheaths. There are bows everywhere—under breast, right shoulder, collar, mid-back, on shoes. The colors represent a tiny slice of the rainbow: blue to Payne's gray, a deep violet-brown, feminine but professional. I gave my girls brilliant Italian paisley silk scarves, rich lavender piping, opals for buttons. For shoes I drew two-inch heels, because these girls don't like to wear sneakers to work.

If I squint, the blue turns tropical, and the edges become lime green and the bows fan orange. I have a metabolic re-action. Resort wear. I can change the colors and increase the flounce and thin the heels and add metallic accents. I can switch the leather bags for rafia, add sunglasses, lighten the linings, imagine a maillot.

And, like the fish in Perdido Pass, I distract myself from the coming storm.

I work until seven. My nine-year-old daughter, Gracie, turns over under her covers. Soon her alarm will buzz. Her father, Bobby, my ex, gave her the alarm after she complained about my waking her up each day. "Mama does it wrong," Gracie told him. I'm sure his face lit up.

I make coffee and take a cup outside.

A few last bats flutter through the air, gulping down Gulf mosquitoes the size of nickels. Stink bugs sit on the flag-stones like tiny chips of granite from the Triassic era. No creature of God wants to eat them. Dried-up cicada hulls litter the driveway, caught in fallen globs of Spanish moss. Acorns and half-eaten pecans thump into the St. Augustine.

I sweep the stoop. The swish of my broom seems like the only sound from here to Louisiana. My mother used to tie plants into her brooms—basil branches, to keep the roaches away; mint, to freshen the kitchen; oleander, to ward off sug-ar ants. Then Sears came out with a man-made fiber broom that didn't make a sound, practically a cotton ball on a stick, and it made my mother feel like the queen of England, she said; which wasn't bad for a scullery maid, she'd add. Our brooms were never scented again.

I grew up in this house. After a dozen years in lower Manhattan, Bobby and I moved back into it, when Rice offered him the epic poetry position. My parents had retired into a nursing home. Gracie has grown up here. I re-papered the rooms. I whitewashed the attic. I put in central air. Then I got rid of Bobby.

My older sister, Lisa, says I'm like those doomed polar bears, genetically programmed to find the original ice floe and hang on while it melts.

A Category 2 hurricane is lumbering toward the Gulf, but the front page of the *Chronicle* is given over to an exhaustive report on the Texans' new quarterback. It is football season, which is everything in Houston. We discuss quarterbacks by their first names. Our universities study artificial turf. People marry under goalposts. We suffered the day the Oilers moved to Tennessee. Thousands of Houstonians held a weepy vigil at the Astrodome the morning our team boarded a bus to go someplace called Nashville, where people thought oil came in cans.

My father lived for football. Played it. Won it. Coached it. Watched it. Then raped my little sister.

I was barely fifteen at the time of Daddy's psychotic break. He raped Claire, beat up my mother, and was then anesthetized to a high-water mark that allowed our family to stay put in the house. For appearances. For disability checks. All thanks to my mother.

The doctors put my father on drugs that made his hair fall out and his personality dissolve. He became a piece of furniture, to save the Calaway family from full-on poverty.

Daddy never surfaced for air again. He existed like a framed certificate on the wall. His football trophies went into boxes in the garage. His perennials died. His car was sold.

Long gone were the days when he would sit on the edge of the sofa, twisting wire coat hangers onto the television antenna and yelling at George Blanda to "throw the damn thing."

"How many of you are there?" he once asked me.

Daddy never realized that Houston got a new football team, and a new stadium, and several new quarterbacks, who also couldn't throw the damn thing.

I go upstairs to check on Gracie. She has Bobby's eyes, cornflower blue, and sometimes when she looks at me in frustration, I see his hatred shining back. Gracie does hate me some for evicting her father. And I hated my mother some for not throwing Daddy out. Swamp-lot karma.

"Do I have to go to school?" Gracie murmurs. She puts two warm tiny arms around my neck. It is heaven. It is that brief moment before she is truly awake and cross with me.

"But you love school," I say, holding her tight.

"But Hurricane Che."

Hurricane Che. Someone at NOAA must have been doubled over with laughter.

"Che hasn't reached Cuba yet," I say. A marvel of a sentence.

"My teacher said Che was a hero because he helped the farmers."

"Really?" I imagine this teacher googling for five minutes to tease an innocuous fact from pages of guerrilla warfare.

"She said Che is an exception to the rule," Gracie says.

"What rule?"

"American names. Are Katrina and Rita American names?"

"I guess." I'm flunking this conversation.

"My teacher said Che gave a lot of people hope."

"Which teacher is this?"

Gracie recoils with annoyance. "You don't care," she mutters.

I toast raisin bread for breakfast and dice apples for a pie. Gracie appears in the kitchen with her eyes half-open. Fourth graders are allowed to wear princess blouses under their plaid jumpers this year, with lilac piping on the collars, and Gracie feels very stylish. She'd been looking forward to fourth-grade uniforms forever, she said. She's got on two different socks and her hair is headed in a variety of directions.

"Emma is evacuating to Paris with her mom," Gracie says. Sniffs.

Emma is her best friend. Emma's mother, MaryJane, went to high school with me and my sisters, seldom acknowledged us, and married well. We've gotten to be good friends because I design dresses that are so expensive only MaryJane can afford them.

"Is Daddy evacuating?" Gracie asks. Her voice has changed into something sharpened.

"I don't know," I say. What do I know? Last week Bobby got into a brawl at The Ginger Man bar, after Rice denied him tenure. The next day his lawyer filed a new child custody suit. I wish Bobby would evacuate Houston forever.

Gracie makes a low sound. "If Daddy goes, I want to go with him. I'm the only kid in the whole school who isn't evacuating."

I open my mouth and nothing comes out. Hurricane Che is massive but wind strength is not catastrophic. The mayor has asked everyone to hunker down. Only Galveston, an oversize sandbar fifty miles to our south, has been told to evacuate.

Gracie growls, "The. Only. One. Staying."

I don't know how to diffuse her. She's ticking. "Maybe MaryJane will take you to Paris," I say.

"I'm allowed to be with Daddy."

Let me go! I wonder.

Gracie grabs an apple and stomps out to the car.

There was a time when little girls could walk to school, could pad along the culverts and hold hands to cross streets and catch geckos in the grass. That liberty faded in the nineties, and a heavy tombstone dropped on it in 2005 when Hurricane Katrina washed the Ninth Ward of New Orleans onto our streets.

Gracie is silent in the car. She is like a small storm in the Atlantic, sucking up the warm air, swirling. But when we pull up at school, her eyes pop open with anticipation. School is play. Education is sugared like grapefruits. The days of force-feeding information to children are over. Under President George Bush the Umpteenth, someone found out that torture doesn't work.

2

Back at home, I throw the diced apples into a pot with brown sugar, white sugar, lemon juice, raisins, and cinnamon. My mother taught me to cook the fruit before setting it into a pie crust. I let the apples reduce on low heat until they become a lumpy brown glistening glop. Brown is what Midwesterners wear, my mother liked to remind us, and they raise pigs.

My mother had so many convictions that I think she used up all of mine. Brown is a thousand shades of beauty—umber, sienna, raw, burnt, sepia, ochre, almond, bronze, camel, dun, chestnut, coffee, taupe. Every color is a potential runway revelation except yellow, which according to M.K. is worn only by Englishwomen.

I slip my pie into the oven.

You wouldn't know a storm was swirling around the Caribbean if you looked out the window. Squirrels drop half-eaten pecans from high branches. My pecan tree is their Luby's Cafeteria and they wander down each branch with the leisure of those with trays.

I'm about to head upstairs to work when the phone rings. Caller ID reads Tranquility Oaks, the nursing home where my father has been passing away for years. Can he have finally thrown in the game?

"Miss Calaway? This is Ramzi, your own Ramzi, from Tranquility Oaks? Your father is here with us?"

"Yes," I say. "Of course, Ramzi. How are you?"

"I am very fine, thank you for asking, Miss Calaway. *Insh'allah.*"

Ramzi is the manager of the life-care facility where my father continues to be dying, where my mother took the fast track. Ramzi is half-Egyptian, half-Mexican, and five thousand percent gay. He dresses in silk organza suits and vivid ties made of the same fabric as the upholstery in the Tranquility's lobby. You can lose him on a sofa.

Thanks to Ramzi, Tranquility Oaks runs like clockwork. He is roundly adored. The old ladies knit him beanies in bright yarn, and he wears them like plumage. When the old men grouse about the car service, Ramzi quivers with outrage and publicly harangues the infidels at the valet desk. In gratitude, Tranquility's residents pass away on a convenient schedule and the painters can come in.

I like Ramzi. He always made it a point to know what football teams my father favored and he mourned grievously when my mother passed away. In fact, he wept alone.

"Oh," he cried, tears bubbling down his smooth cheeks. "She was here too short a time. Such a delight, your mother, and she was so happy here! La! La! La!"

A delight? My mother? But certainly she had been happy at Tranquility Oaks. She'd waited all her life for this high-rise to heaven. Here were all the amenities and creature comforts she'd never had. Central air conditioning, prepared meals, floors polished not by yours truly, one's own television, and best of all, a bed of her own.

Once, remarkably, my mother conceded that if God were going to forgive all those Arabs, then she hoped Ramzi could cut to the front of the line. I grew up hearing about the crowds in heaven. Is it really heaven if you can't find a chair? "People just keep dying!" my mother used to huff, zipping up her black dress for another wine and cheese service at Bradshaw-Carter's funeral home.

This morning Ramzi says, "Miss Calaway, I am calling with regard to your father."

My father, soon-to-be graduate of Ramzi's curriculum. A few months ago, they rushed Daddy to the hospital, and then to hospice as we watched his vital signs sink. But Daddy recovered to an extent impossible to ignore, and Ramzi was forced to take him back to Tranquility Oaks. That's what a life-care contract guarantees. You give them all your money and they take care of you until your last goodnight.

My father's room had already been co-opted, so Ramzi was forced to install him in the Briar Suite, an airy corner room overlooking the courtyard and set aside for the who's-who of Houston elderly. It had Victorian settees in lilac, matching silk drapes, built-in bookshelves, and a walnut coffee table on wheels. Not that Daddy was aware of his luck. You could count on one hand the residents of Tranquility Oaks who were in a position to make observations about their rooms.

On the day they wheeled my father's gurney into the Briar Suite, I had an inkling that Ramzi's honeyed affection for us was drying up. The Calaways were not playing cricket.

"Miss Calaway," he declares this morning. "I am pained to make this phone call. We are like family now, la? Your sweet mother, may she rest in peace, was a gift to all of us."

A squeak escapes me.

"Miss Calaway, we are in the initial stages of preparing for the hurricane. May God forbid it tracks straight to our beloved city, but in case the worst happens, we will be evacuating our residents to Dallas. Insh'allah."

"Dallas is nice," I say.

"We are blessed to have accommodations in all emergencies. Unfortunately, Miss Calaway, and this wrenches my soul, we cannot take your father with us. He has signed a Refusal to Evacuate form. Legally, I cannot put this delightful man on our bus. La."

I feel time slam on the brakes.

"A *what* form?"

"Refusal to Evacuate. Technically Form 31B." Ramzi suddenly sounds like a British solicitor. There is a rustle of paper. "Ah…blah, blah, blah…under no circumstances shall said resident be party to evacuation…blah, blah, blah. I have it here in my hand. I should tear it up, it is breaking my heart so."

"My father held a pen and signed a piece of paper?"

"Oh, but this was years ago."

"There's a date?"

"Yes. Let me see. September of 2017. If you recall, during the Rita evacuation, a bus on Interstate 45, just short of Dallas, caught fire, and—I can hardly recount it—all the passengers were taken by angels. Because of this tragedy, Miss Calaway, nursing homes across the good state of Texas are compelled to have Form 31B on file. And here it is."

"But where will he go?"

"Let me think, Miss Calaway. Short of municipal geriatric centers, you mean? Or the county shelter? Perhaps to your home?"

I gasp.

"Your father might be better off at home," he concludes.

"Here? My house?" I think I'll black out. I'm in a delirium of no.

Ramzi's voice. "It was before, I believe, your father's house? How special."

"But, Ramzi, this is just a house. It's not outfitted for a nursing home patient."

"I am happy to recommend two other private facilities, run by very capable people, very good friends of mine. However, these applications take time, and...well."

"Ramzi, this form that my father signed."

"Yes."

"I don't remember it."

"It is a great fault in the system," Ramzi moans empathetically. "The paperwork is overwhelming. Our good legislature is constantly adding to our burdens."

I feel partially paralyzed, a fish stick halfway through the flash-freezing process.

Ramzi says, "I'm pained to admit there is one other wrinkle, Miss Calaway. You see, once we discharge your father from our care, he must reapply to be readmitted."

"What?" I grab the kitchen counter.

"The rules that govern life-care facilities are ridiculous,

Miss Calaway. Formal discharge, formal admission. You must understand that we delight in having your father stay with us. We are humbled and proud. And when he fills out the application, you can be sure Ramzi will put him on the top of the waiting list."

"He can't just come back after the storm?"

"It is impossible."

The floor is flying up at me.

"Miss Calaway, your father will be so happy to be home. Certainly we all wish to pass to eternal glory from the bosom of our own family. Here is the diamond hidden within the rock. It is we, here, who will be wretched. We will miss your father terribly."

"Wait. Wait. Ramzi, what if the storm doesn't track toward Houston? Then can my father stay at Tranquility Oaks?"

"Naturally, Miss Calaway. This call is only to advise you of the possibility. However, I must tell you I am under great pressure to issue the evacuation order, you can understand, to make things as smooth as possible for our guests."

In that instant, I know that Ramzi is going to lower the ax on my father.

"Would you like to come pick him up, Miss Calaway?"

"You mean, in case?"

"In case. Of course."

"I don't…"

"Of course I can have someone bring him home to you."

"Probably a better…"

"Shall we say Wednesday morning then?"

"In case."

There's an electronic ping on his end of the line. "Oh!" Ramzi exclaims. "Miss Calaway, I have just received on my screen a directive from our parent company to proceed with evacuation. How timely. Well, we're all settled then. May I say again that we have enjoyed yourself and your family! And yet, I feel peace in my heart that your father is going home."

His voice simply stops, vanishes, like a candle quenched.

He's hung up. I imagine him striding down his silk-striped hallways, dusting his hands of an irksome burr—that Calaway clan—for tying up his beloved Briar Suite.

3

My father acquired this house from Bisskit, his mother-in-law I grew up here, Claire was raped here, and when my parents moved into Tranquility Oaks, they left it to me by default. Claire had disappeared from their lives. My older sister, Lisa, is a banking mogul in New York City. She escaped this house just after The Mess, and it remains, for her, a shack that fell far, far from the yellow brick road. "You come with the house, Julia! You're like a light fixture," she says.

The very bruised Claire never quite disappeared from my life. She's an artist in New York City. She hates this house and her family with a passion that is inspiring. *Fuck you, Julia.* Inspiring to her. I'm on her side. She had to live in this house while her father-rapist shuffled around in his pajamas and talked to the air. The quality of her fury is epic. It splashes across her monumental canvases on large brushes heaped with black and red paint.

Bobby, my ex, hated this house from the moment our battered old Volvo lurched into the driveway five years ago. Bright green geckos skittered across the broken blocks of concrete, and fat fronds of ironweed brushed at our tires.

"You missed the exit for Houston," Bobby grumbled. "You drove us to Nicaragua." Gifting to Gracie a solid hatred for this old house.

After Bobby left, as per a county restraining order, Gracie saw the sagging floorboards and coarse St. Augustine grass the way Lisa and Claire did—manifestations of an abandoned jail. It's only the two of us now who track grit into the kitchen, eat enchiladas at the old pine table in the kitchen, and tape photographs and cartoons on the walls. Gracie, even in the throes of her pain from the divorce, slides down the banister the way I once did. She changes clothes eight times a day, the way I did. She makes collages using whole bottles of glue. The way I used to. If a house could be bored to death by its occupants, then this one would be a pile of rubble.

During the last year of my marriage I was introduced to this house's flintier sides when Bobby smacked me into stairs and cabinets. One time he pushed me so hard I toppled down the last few steps of the staircase and blacked out on the foyer floor. In that instant, when the blackness crept from the edges of my sight, and a scream burst noiselessly from my lips, I had an insight into the brutal incident that destroyed Claire's life forever. I used to wish she would just move on; but I saw the pure impossibility of it then. You are one creature, on one journey, and violence marks your gait for good.

I didn't know how Claire managed, but I bought a gun.

The oven timer beeps a creepy grim knell. Blistering on the middle rack is the Honeycrisp pie I baked for Mrs. Berry next door. Her mother, whom everyone called Sugar, just died at the age of ninety-six. We grew up alongside the Berrys, the three skinned-knees Calaway girls tussling out childhood with the three juvie Berry boys. Our Indians to their cowboys. Our base-stealers to their ball-whackers. Our interesting breasts to their interesting penises.

Sugar died in a head-on car collision four days ago. She was killed on her way to Memorial City Mall by an eighteen-wheeler with Quintana Roo plates, driven by a dog-tired old drunk, who crossed the median strip. It's not easy to cross the median strip on Interstate 10, because there's a four-foot concrete wall where the grass should be. There's concrete where most grass should be in Houston.

I couldn't help but think how frightened Mrs. Berry's mother must have been, seeing the huge truck explode toward her in a billow of dust and rock and steel. She was so tiny and crooked over with osteoporosis. Standing beside her closed casket I had to unfurl her in my mind. The obituary said she'd been a trophy barrel-racer once, Miss Teen-age Cotton Queen, president of the Junior League, and a national runner-up in the Pillsbury bake-off of 1984. At a certain age, you begin to get acquainted with people at their memorial services.

I cool the pie on a rack on the kitchen counter. The rack is heavy, blackened iron, rusted in spots and bent at the corners, something you might lay down to set concrete. Bisskit brought it with her from South Carolina, all that time ago, when her second husband took a job in the oil patch and moved the family down to Houston. When I put my nose to its ripply grid, I swear I can smell buttermilk biscuits again.

Several cars are parked in front of the Berrys'. I break a sweat walking over with the pie. September beats August in the tropical misery department. Geckos dart left and right out of my path, neon-green stunners and those dung-colored ones. It's family season for geckos, and babies flicker across the ground like quicksilver.

Mrs. Berry greets me at the door, her eyes rimmed in red, her lower lip twitching. She has forgone makeup, which is unlike her. There are flowers everywhere—on tables, shelves and chairs, and even on the floor, lining the little foyer. Tall white calla lilies, red roses cinched by colored twine, mixed bouquets, hydrangea dyed cemetery-mauve. A kindly woman swoops over and takes my pie to the kitchen. Mrs. Berry clutches me to her squishy bosom.

"Thank you, darling Julia," she says. "You just grow more beautiful every day. Come in and meet my friends."

I follow her into her living room, which is as familiar as my own.

"This is Julia Calaway," Mrs. Berry announces to the room of women, all of whom are Mrs. Berry's age. All of whom are longstanding Houstonians who remember some hideous Calaway story. One is in a wheelchair, with an afghan over her knees. Another is adjusting her glasses with a palsied hand. They all look beaten to the bone.

"Julia grew up next door," Mrs. Berry says. There is an unflattering rustle of appreciation. "You girls had all the luck, the longest legs and the prettiest faces in Houston. My boys used to go cross-eyed when those Calaway girls were in the yard."

"We played in the yard whenever Sugar pulled out her baking pans," I say to her. The Berrys always made extra for the Calaway girls.

Mrs. Berry hugs me to her. "I'm making a book of Sugar's recipes. I told her about it this summer, and she was so excited about that book. 'Did you get the catfish Veracruz?' she asked me. 'Yes, Mom. I got the catfish Veracruz and the catfish Monterrey and the catfish fried nice.'"

Nice, recipe-wise, meant breaded.

Mrs. Berry adds, "She asked to include your grandmother's biscuit recipe. Bisskit wrote it out for her once. She was honest about her recipes."

Bisskit got her nickname when she was only six years old. She'd shown uncommon zeal for hacking cold Crisco into flour and salt, and dribbling in some buttermilk and producing flaky biscuits that seemed to heal the day. The spelling was on account of kindergarten being the sum total of her scholarship.

In Mrs. Berry's kitchen, dozens more vases explode with flowers. She pulls out a shoebox of handwritten recipes and flips through the cards with a practiced thumb.

"Thank you for that nice pie, Julia," Mrs. Berry says. "How is your daddy?"

"Fine." I blanch. "Good."

"Jack and I are fixing to drive to the ranch tomorrow. Early evacuation and all that. You and Gracie could come on out and stay with us."

"Thank you, Mrs. Berry. I think we're going to hunker down."

"I might, at your age. But Jack hates hurricanes." She wipes away rogue tears with the back of a sleeve. "You know something? With Sugar dying, I suddenly feel abandoned to my marriage. Like there's no buffer anymore. Not that I don't love Jack. I do. But Sugar made it easier to be alive. Julia, take some of these flowers back to your house. I'd have to rent an eighteen-wheeler to get them all out to the ranch."

Eighteen-wheelers. Quintana Roo plates. The image makes our eyes well up.

"I'm so sorry about your loss, Mrs. Berry. We all loved Sugar."

"She did love you girls, too. She wanted to take you all in, you know, after the unhappiness. Then we heard Lisa was packing for boarding school—she was crackerjack bright, that Lisa—and, well, it didn't seem right to trespass on your family. You all got through it in the end. Nobody gets off scot-free." She looks at me with the kindest kind of pity.

"No," I say. I want to ask about the boys, but I know one is in Iraq, one is in prison, and the third fishes in the Gulf. The Berrys didn't get off scot-free, and it's a mystery how trouble can seek out the most bighearted parents.

She hands me a recipe card. It is cornmeal-yellow with age and stained with something brown, probably black coffee, which Bisskit drank like an addict. I wonder whether, having dripped coffee on the recipe card, Bisskit considered getting a fresh one. But Bisskit grew up during the Great Depression, in an inarticulate community that saved the labels from tinned peas for writing paper.

2 C flowor, C butter milk. The pen virtually grinding ink into the cardstock because Bisskit had a tremor toward the end, and she fought it off with a steely will, her fingers resisting domination, "making an Alamo out of it," she said. I remember watching her use an embroidery needle with demonic resolution. Her fingers hovered above the canvas, then impaled it. Blood speckled the backing.

My fingers explore the deep embossing of Bisskit's scrawl.

"Thank you for this," I say. "It's precious."

"Your mother once told me about growing up in the Pee Dee. A sharecropper's child who spent her childhood in the back seat of an old station wagon. She said Bisskit made a little bed for her and Loretta, and the girls curled up next to the family scythes."

Mrs. Berry takes my hand and walks with me to the door. "You've had a road, Julia. And I know you scrapped the whole God thing long ago. But I like to think my mother is in a prettier place, you know? And I like to think I'll join her one day."

"If there's a heaven, Mrs. Berry, you'll both be there." No queue for them, I thought. She and Sugar were God's reward for all his days of hard work.

"I'm going to let myself think that you'll join us, too, some day," Mrs. Berry says.

I give her a last, sad embrace. Sad is a suburb. My mother never once said she hoped to see me in eternity.

Outside, it is Baghdad hot and Gulf Coast wet. Only a succulent could love it. The air is so thick that the mosquitoes just hang in it. Grendel's own cicadas are shrieking. My ex, Bobby-the-Hitter, told me Grendel was descended from Cain. I once asked my mother if she'd heard about this during her forays into the Catholic church, but Father Pat hadn't sermonized about Grendel. Father Pat felt literature was something that fizzled out during the 1960s.

My mother embraced the Catholic church after Bisskit died. Maybe she, too, suddenly felt abandoned to her marriage, finding herself alone with three little girls and a husband, whose best day ever was December 12, 1951, when he threw 147 yards for three touchdowns at a high school that closed.

My mother shopped her churches. St. Vincent's, St. Paul's, the downtown cathedral. She landed on St. Vincent's. St. Vincent's had nicer pews, she said. St. Vincent's had a better organ. St. Vincent's had air conditioning. And one day, "St. Vincent's has better holy wafers."

Lisa's face lit up. She was twelve at the time. "Let's us make the best church wafers in Texas!"

We were electrified by the idea. We baked hundreds of paper-thin sugar cookies. We hawked them up and down the street looking for reactions. Claire decorated boxes with what she said were Roman Catholic symbols. Lisa made up a sales ledger. I baked and baked. We were fixing to be millionaires. Even our mother marked her interest by not screaming at us to get out of the kitchen. After weeks of experimentation, we had our perfect wafer, and a cereal box painted white and decorated with genderless cherubs. My mother took this to Father Pat at St. Vincent's and he shook his head and said that Catholic wafers were consecrated by the Holy Roman mob and baked in consecrated kitchens.

Our mother sulked for days. If we'd been cats, we'd have been kicked.

4

Mrs. Berry sends me home with armfuls of lilies that drench the house with their perfume. As I bring some sheets downstairs to the washing machine, I feel like a bat—my senses overwhelmed by odors. The lilies get moved to the dining room. I consider closing the door on them, but love for Mrs. Berry stops me. Maybe the lilies are like fallen pennies, things that turn up to make you stop and reconsider. Or maybe they're just a friendly reminder of how immoderate life is. Like hurricanes.

Someone would do well to pinch me. I can't seem to remember that I have work to do. The Pitti Palazzo showroom in New York is in crisis mode. Leona Milana will be eating Chinese takeout by the boxful. M.K. will be scarfing vitamin B and Xanax from the jellybean bowl.

M.K. calls as I walk into my attic studio.

"Julia," he says. "It's like National Mourning Day here. Tell me you've got something gorgeous on your walls or I'll go *poof*."

I flip the switch and observe my ladies.

"Are you still drawing on the walls, Julia?"

"I am."

"You make me want to design wallpaper, baby."

"I'll send you jpegs today, M.K. I can have the specs done by the end of this week."

"Yesterday would be good, baby. These Italians, they're always screaming, you know? They're noisy."

The models waltzing up and down my walls right now are thinking about global affairs. They work in think tanks. They sue polluters. They write op-eds about Crimea, the Paris Accord, and public school funding. They're not smiling.

Indanthrone blue, Payne's gray, dawn-colored gimp tied into bows along the shoulder. Starched silk bows like mini-obis in a line down the back. Mauve against blues. Pale blues against deep grays. Taking an oil stick, I draw and smudge lines, modifying a figure in full stride. She has one foot carefully forward and her arms out, almost as though she's lost her balance. But I would never let it happen.

I love my women, each one slightly different, bemused, unhurried but never stopping. When Gracie was little she liked to climb onto a chair and crayon smiles on them. When Bobby left, she would use an oil stick and draw rivers of tears on their faces.

I work for hours, then photograph the models next to fabric swatches. I email the JPEGs to New York and go downstairs to grab a late lunch. The lilies wasted no time waging war on my sinuses. Squatters. I love Mrs. Berry, but the lilies are going to the garage. That's how I notice the garage doors are open. A hot breeze drifts through the bays. I realize that my father's arrival, on the cusp of a hurricane, has left me just a little in shock.

At three, it's time to collect Gracie from school. Out inspecting her roses is my neighbor Mimi Blanton, of the original Blanton clan, which in Houston is synonymous with unimaginable oil riches and genetic Republicanism. Mrs. Blanton is nearly seventy years old, but she looks younger than me. Her smile is a little wider than a soap dish.

"Good afternoon, Julia!" she warbles, waving a many-bangled wrist to flag me down. "I'm having the roses pruned and fertilized today. Mid-September and mid-February, every year. I apologize preemptively for any debris that blows onto your yard." She sails across her lawn in white slacks and a striped Chanel blouse with twenty-two karat buttons. Her ballet flats match. She wears massive Jackie-O sunglasses, making me wistful for the old bipartisan days of fashion.

"It's no problem, Mrs. Blanton," I said, smiling. I have

called her Mrs. Blanton since I was three years old, and she will never suggest I called her Mimi.

"Your eyes are a bit bloodshot, darling," Mrs. Blanton says.

"Paint," I nod, rubbing them.

"We're throwing a little party Wednesday evening to welcome DeBeers to the Galleria."

"That's nice of you."

"It's the least we can do. They've just lost a class-action lawsuit for price-fixing, and the plunge in oil prices is killing them." She clicks her tongue. "Whatever you say about Nixon, he wouldn't have put us here."

I clear my throat because I'm not sure what that meant.

I sometimes think Mimi Blanton will give up the fight and put concertina wire between her five-lot estate and everyone else's more modest proposal. She doesn't engage with anyone else on the street—although Judge Garwood presided over her first two divorces—but she keeps up with me because I design clothing that her daughters adore.

"My girls will be wearing Pitti at the party," Mrs. Blanton adds, making my ears burn red.

"I'm flattered." I almost feel invited, especially because "the girls" (all three now mothers) beg me to come alter something—let out a side seam, narrow a dart—minutes before every party. They squabble with each other like fussy toddlers, which is almost enough to make me feel fortunate about my childhood. Which is cause for review.

We grew up next door to these sisters, but we never played together. They were shipped off to finishing schools on the East Coast before The Mess in our house. Sometimes on a mild evening, I sit on my front stoop with a glass of cold wine, and while the heat and humidity give me a facial, I'll hear Mrs. Blanton scream like a barn owl from across her rose gardens, and I wonder whether, if we had screamed more at one another, the worst would never have happened.

Did Claire scream? Would it have mattered?

"I'm leaving town just as soon as the last DeBeers walks out my door," Mrs. Blanton says. "You and I, darling, we're too old for hurricanes." *Ouch.* "The last time we lost power," she recalls, "I had my man discard the contents of two refrigerators. Four leaf bags full of spoiled food and six syringes of epinephrine. Then the lawn men found the bags in the garage and ate the spoiled food and injected themselves with the epinephrine, which they must have thought was something nice, like heroin. Fortunately they were illegals, so they couldn't sue us." She reviews her bangles. "At least sedatives are effective at room temperature."

"How is Jesse?" I ask Mrs. Blanton.

Mrs. Blanton's current husband, Jesse, is in commercial real estate. He's made a fortune from Houston's recent upswing, and he's running for mayor to make sure nobody slows him down.

"Everybody's voting for Jesse," Mrs. Blanton smiles, lips curving into a machete.

Jesse's opponent come November is a Democratic trial lawyer and the first Jew allowed to buy land on River Oaks Boulevard. His name is Hugie Feldman and he made a pile of money from the silicone breast implant class-action lawsuit. People admire moneymaking here in Houston almost as much as they admire a well-turned breast, but they prefer the Star of Texas to the Star of David.

"That lawyer man is a goner," Mrs. Blanton adds. "Couldn't get himself voted dogcatcher in Del Rio."

She checks her watch. It's so encrusted with diamonds that I get sun shards in my eyes. "Time to meet with the caterers," she says. "You'll stop by, won't you, Wednesday night, to snip any threads?"

"Of course," I say and then I realize that my father will be delivered that same morning, and I begin to make hesitating noises—ers and ums, which go unnoticed.

"By the way, Bobby is looking well," Mrs. Blanton says. "Every marriage needs a brush with divorce to stay fresh."

I wave goodbye to Mrs. Blanton, who raises her eyebrows in reply. Where on earth would she have seen Bobby?

5

I don't know how I ended up married to Bobby. The violence crept into our marriage gradually, almost stealthily. At first I felt humiliated, then frightened and disgusted, and later I even pitied myself. I spewed out excuses the way toads spew out eggs. Denial was built into my system. I let it last too long because leaving Bobby referenced a deeper failure, like maybe choosing Bobby. Bisskit used to say about her marriage: she ordered the meatloaf and no one warned her what the sides would be.

Bobby's primary response to the divorce was rage. Well, it was his primary, secondary, and tertiary response.

"You ruined everything!" he shouted at me. Even at the courthouse he advanced on me. A policeman grabbed him by the arm and at that instant I burst into tears of relief. Might someone really protect me? I fell to my knees on the courthouse marble.

But the policemen were not always there. Bobby was ordered to stay away from me and Gracie, but he liked to call from strange phones with vague threats and unsettling threats. Rice put him on probation. I felt terrible because I never meant to jeopardize his work. People divorce. I'd hoped the whole thing would slip quietly into history.

The calls became less frequent, but one morning I found my tires slashed. And there was the time he picked Gracie up from school and took her up to Dallas with him for a medieval English conference. He left Gracie in the hotel room with a key to the minibar and an all-clear on renting movies. She had the presence of mind to call and tell me. He brought her home two days later.

There was the broken window. There were the smashed

flower pots. There were bitter emails. Then, just this past May as I came home from driving Gracie to school, the house was ringed with fire trucks from Ladder Co. 16. They had their lights blazing and a dozen men were combing our property. No flames were licking from the windows. I'd hardly been gone twenty minutes.

I pulled tentatively into the driveway. A fireman with a badge was hosing off a big galvanized steel trashcan on the side lawn. He looked vaguely familiar. The smell of burnt metal and plastic and newsprint was everywhere.

"This is my house," I said.

"We got an alarm about fifteen minutes ago," the fireman explained. "Someone lit papers in this trashcan. Whoever it was, he was a moron. He did it right near the smoke alarm. You're lucky."

"Where exactly was it?"

"Kitchen." He tipped his head. "Are you Claire's sister?"

"Uh-oh," I said. This kind of admission never boded well.

He laughed. "I should have known. You Calaway girls were magnets for trouble."

"You're thinking of Lisa and Claire." Throw the absent ones under the bus.

"I went to high school with Claire," he said. "She wasn't there much."

"She's an artist now."

"Bet her canvases aren't easy on the eye."

No point in telling him about the torn women, the silent screams, the immolated shadow-figures. I said, "What happened to Claire… It was past terrible. She couldn't help what she became."

He nodded. "I see a lot of bad things. I never tell people they'll get over it."

That was the day I realized I might have to kill Bobby. The length and breadth of my vulnerability seemed to be expanding infinitely, like the universe. No one would step in to protect me and Gracie. I'd exhausted my legal options.

Locking my doors and breathing deeply wasn't enough to keep Bobby from our home.

I picked up Gracie from school that afternoon and hugged her tightly and said, "I love you so much."

She said, "Uh-oh."

6

This house has seen its fair share of guns. Bisskit had a gun that her second husband used on the day he called it quits. We called it "the blunderbuss" because it was big and awkward and inaccurate to a fault unless, as our step-Grandpa demonstrated, you put it in your mouth.

My father had his hunting rifles, eight sleek, oiled beauties that he kept in a cherry cabinet with a glass front. My mother sold them for a nickel after The Mess, when the doctors put Daddy on a diet of pills, and he lost his hair and his mind and then his eyesight too.

There were no guns in this house when I moved in with Bobby, and none on the day I threw the last of Bobby's things out a second-floor window. The gun came later, when the glimmers of Bobby's instability turned into bright lights.

It's easy to buy a weapon. I drove southwest on 59 to Fondren, a street in Houston brimming with dicey things—cheap furniture, cheap prostitutes, food made in China, pawned cars, and gun ranges with vending machines that sell bullets and self-piercing kits. In a strip mall near Westheimer is the Houston Gun Factory Outlet. Randall Kuykendahl, Proprietor.

Randall looked like Santa of the stout belly, apple-cheeks, and curly white facial hair, but he spoke like Goering of the let's-weed-out-the-weak-ones mold. Randall was a retired Harris County sheriff with three ex-wives and five daughters, who wouldn't talk to him.

"Go figure," he reflected. "What brings you here?"

I told him.

"You're not the first."

"Does that mean it's legitimate?"

"No. They'll haul your ass to the county lockup if it looks premeditated. Most of the ladies think they've mapped it out real good but in the heat of the moment they don't think so straight. Scrap the plan. Got children?"

"Possibly."

"I'd think hard about this."

"I have."

"Well, I'm not one to refuse a sale." He led me over to his rack room. A poster on the wall declared: Open Season on Democrats. A framed portrait of George Bush and Dick Cheney hung above the counter. I checked my watch to see what year it was.

"Have an idea about the kind of gun you're looking for?" Randall asked.

"No."

"Ever shot a gun?"

"No."

"Ever held a gun?"

"No."

"Well, we know where to start then."

Randall taught me about the different options. Handguns, which the city of Chicago had tried to ban, beckoned me. There were millions to choose from, and they all looked alike, oily and black and heavy, reminding me of Bisskit's cast-iron pans. Randall put one in my hands and explained about triggers and bullets, and after that he walked me over to the shooting range. He put noise-canceling earphones on both of us. Then he showed me how to stand, feet akimbo, how to hold my arms, where to put my fingers, how to draw a bead on a target.

"Do the little ones not have crosshairs?" I asked.

"The little whats?" he frowned.

"The little guns?"

"Did you want a rifle?"

"No. No. This is perfect. I just thought there would be crosshairs."

He nodded toward the target, an outline of a person on paper. "Aim for the heart. Where that red dot is."

"Shouldn't the dot be a little to the right?" I asked, the gun slipping in my grip as my palms began to sweat.

"People are dumb-asses about anatomy."

"I can't do this," I whimpered.

"This is real life."

"But this," I said, letting the gun dangle between my thumb and forefinger for one second before Randall grabbed it with an expression like terror. "I was thinking of a wounding type of gun. You know, for scaring someone off."

He stared at me. "Nobody shoots to wound."

"I came here thinking about, you know, getting rid of… But now with a gun in my hand… Well, your hand now… I'm thinking maybe just to scare him off."

Randall stared at me.

"I'm a coward," I said.

For the next two hours I test-drove guns, sweating completely through my shirt and crying out only once, when a gun's kickback pitched me backwards onto the concrete floor. We finally fixed on a model, a Sig-something. I brought the gun home and removed it from the car using oven mitts. Then I moved into the guest room (because Randall said I had to switch beds to take a killer by surprise. Wasn't I supposed to be the killer?). I put the gun in the bedside table and laid the oven mitts on top of it and stuffed the box of ammunition in the back of my underwear drawer. Then I threw up.

After a few weeks, I resented the gun's proximity and moved it to the top shelf of the old built-ins with its heavy box of bullets. Within the month I moved back into the master bedroom. I just didn't have the staying power for murder. I didn't have the assassin's patience and just possibly I began to lose interest in my polychromatic revenge. My boring life seeped back in through the cracks. Purple was going to be big and M.K. was rearranging more cans in his cupboard. It was summer. I took Gracie to Galveston to hunt for hermit crabs. I drew dress designs for Pitti Palazzo's winter 2019 collection. The markets were up and I added mink fringe to hems. Sometimes I thought about that gun, sitting up on the highest shelf of the guest room collecting dust. It had become a household god, an idol for warding off evil intruders by the fact of its being, and a couple of times I sent it short prayers, and once I came very close to naming it.

7

Gracie is glowering in the school's roundabout when I pull up. I manage to nick the curb for a nice brain-scrambling jolt.

"You're late, Mama."

"Hi, Gracie. I'm so glad to see you, and I'm sorry to be late."

"Well, I had a bad day."

"Can you tell me about it?"

"You want me to re-live it?"

I blow a little air out through my lips. We get underway.

"Could you try to miss one pothole?" Gracie snaps.

At home, I cut up some nectarines, grapes, and plums for her.

"Everybody's evacuating for the hurricane except us," she says.

"Not everybody, I think. The mayor and the judge have advised us to hunker down with supplies. It's only Category 2 right now."

"Everybody."

"Gracie, your Grandpa is going to come stay with us for a while. A little while. Maybe just a few days. I don't know."

"Why?" she says. She scratches an old bug bite with one hand while she fishes for grapes with the other.

"He just needs to be home for a bit."

"What room is his?"

"I'm not sure yet." I watch her stare indolently out the window as she chews.

"Do you think Daddy will get married again?" Gracie asks.

I am slow to answer. "I don't know."

"You don't know, or you don't want to tell me?" she growls.

"I don't know, Gracie. And staring at someone doesn't make them change their story."

"Sometimes it does. With my friends it does."

I pull out my second bag of Honeycrisps. "I'm going to make your favorite pie. Maybe that will brighten your day."

She looks on with no intimation that it might.

Lisa was the seed that would fracture granite to grow. As a child, she divided the world into "Those who drive me where I want to go" and "The damned." All summer she would swim at the Shamrock Hotel pool. "Don't you dare pick me up before nine p.m.!" she yelled to our mother, racing away from the car with a beach towel under one arm and a bag of tanning gels under the other. She was going to catch the eye of an oilman and live rich.

Lisa got the first air-conditioning unit in the house because she was the squeakiest wheel, and she would cant its louvers straight down and lie on her rag rug moaning with relief while it rattled against the windowsill and shook out cold slabs of air. Claire and I were allowed to play Scrabble on her bed if we promised not to raise the room temperature with our body heat. Then my parents got an air-conditioning unit installed in their bedroom, and later one for the downstairs, where it was never unbearable anyway. Finally Claire and I got window units for our bedrooms, and we all closed our doors and slept like bears and found we'd become nicer people both for the physical comforts and for not having to interact with each other.

"Lisa could be a nurse. She's got the brains for it," our mother said, starching and ironing our pillowcases so that they crunched under our heads. "In a hospital, you can have a nose like that. Claire got the beauty, but she'll squander it."

My mother's *Book of Options for Girls* fit in the margins of a sales receipt.

Lisa dragged us into each new decade. She made me hem her skirts to within an inch of their zippers. They were so popular at school, she made a small business of it, giving me a dollar per skirt and refusing to tell me her profits.

Our mother shrieked when she saw these skirts. "Only whores wear clothes like that!"

"You told me to be enterprising," Lisa screamed back. "Because you said my nose isn't going to get me into show business."

In the end, Lisa proved she was enterprising. She got an MBA from Harvard and a big job in New York City. Over the years, she's flirted with plastic surgery for her nose, but each time, after staring into the mirror for an innermost goodbye, she has retreated. It's only when you try to perfect yourself that you realize it involves a small scrap of suicide, and that the parts of you that always seemed at fault, were anyway defining; if you disposed of your nose, you were choosing someone else, not you, to be.

I stir the sugar into the cooking apples and dial Lisa, to bring her up to date. Just months ago when Lisa was here, we visited Daddy at hospice. She made her goodbyes and then said, "I don't trust him dying." She said Daddy was like a left defensive tackle—primed to nail you even when you had a foot in the end zone.

She was right. Daddy threw his vehicle into "Reverse" when he saw that "Drive" was taking him straight to the morgue. They had to ship him back to Tranquility Oaks. Hospice ought to have put a ONE WAY sign on the front of his door and a WRONG WAY sign on the inside of it. Daddy always obeyed a good sign.

Cool as a cucumber, Lisa listens to my news about Daddy. "You are shitting me!" she screams. "When?"

"Tomorrow." Nothing. "Are you still there, Lisa?" I ask.

"I'm here. I might've blacked out a sec."

I imagine her in her New York City office overlooking

Sixth Avenue, high off the ground and surrounded by massive columns of success. She adds, "Honestly, I'd rather engage in hideously bitter litigation. What can I do for you, Julia? I'm going to send you a check, first of all. You'll need to hire help. Call the River Oaks Temp Agency. They've been around forever. Next, I'm going to sue the bricks off Tranquility Oaks. Let me find out who the corporate parent is...."

I hear her nails clicking on computer keys.

"You don't think I can handle this?" I ask.

"I don't think Mother Teresa could handle this. You can't take Daddy into your home without help. You're not a nurse. And Daddy should be in a jail anyway, not in anyone's home. This is truly bizarre. I was just down there. We thought he only had a few hours left, remember? He was lying in the hospice bed, sleeping and drooling like everybody else. An X-rated movie would have euthanized him."

"If he's just going to lie still," I say, "I can manage."

"And if he doesn't lie still? I know that sounds nuts, but... You need to hire an aide."

"Lisa, no one is looking for employment a few days before a hurricane."

Lisa is quiet a sec. "You're expecting a hurricane?"

"Che."

"Che? As in the Marxist revolutionary? Someone in Washington DC has a sense of humor? When is the storm due?"

"Friday."

"Well, one two three four five. Here's the deal," Lisa says firmly. "I'm going to call the River Oaks Temp Agency right now, and you will be interviewing candidates tomorrow afternoon. I'm sorry to lay this on you, but I just can't buzz down there today. I'm waiting on a big announcement. Hey, does Gracie know?"

"She's been told. I don't know that either of us anticipates reality well."

"If Daddy were moving in with me," Lisa snorts, "reality would be the last thing I'd want to anticipate. I don't even know…is he still on all those medications? Are you supposed to administer medications? I am fucking falling off my chair, Julia."

I turn off the burner underneath the apples. A chill sweeps through me.

Daddy moving into this house with Gracie and me.

Claire was only fourteen when Daddy, in the jaws of a psychotic episode, walked into her room and raped her on her little bed. He was sent to a jail in Bellaire, and my mother turned up in the emergency room with massive bruising and symptoms of an overdose. Amid the utter catastrophe of our lives, the headmaster of St. John's School negotiated a full and immediate scholarship for Lisa at a place called Miss Porter's, somewhere up in New England. Two weeks later we were at the downtown bus stop, dodging grifters and recoiling from air brakes and trying to keep windblown grit out of our eyes. Fritos bags sailed in the wake of passing cars. Our mother, pale and silent as a zombie, put Lisa on a bus that looked like a big milk box. Lisa carried a suitcase full of starched, pressed clothing.

"Just because you're on scholarship doesn't mean you dress like a cracker," our mother mumbled, by way of saying goodbye.

I cried for days. I think I cried for months.

Lisa's beloved voice comes back on the line. "I cannot believe this, Julia. I am so going to sue that Egyptian flamer."

I sigh, pull some shrimp from the refrigerator.

"Forget it. I'm flying down there," Lisa says resolutely. "I'll come help you with this. I'll be there Thursday around noon."

"No. No, Lisa. You're sweet to offer, but we'll be fine. I'll keep you informed."

Lisa makes an anguished noise. "Julia, it's just that I'm due for this promotion."

"No! Another one? If they keep promoting you, won't you be president soon?"

"I'll be retired soon," she says. "Please, please tell me if I can do anything? Wait till Claire hears about this." Lisa whistles.

I get a strange tightening across my shoulders. "Are you two in touch?"

Lisa laughs ruefully. "Define 'in touch.'"

"How is she?" My heart squeezes into a tight fist.

"Claire? She's fine. She's still mucking around the lower West Side. Her old meat locker, the dump she bought for fifty thousand, is worth about five million right now. But she won't sell it, because technically she couldn't be a starving artist then. She had a gallery opening last week. Her paintings make Guernica look like a Labor Day picnic. She's painting blood-red and scab-black bows on her female's privates now, and they're selling like hotcakes."

"Bows?" I gasp. I think about my drawings in the attic.

"Bows. Anyway, how's my favorite Gracie? I miss that sweet baby."

I close my eyes. "Gracie's fine, great, wonderful. She's been told Che Guevara was a farmer."

"Ha! That's rich! Julia, don't you think it's funny how you threw Bobby out after all those years and now you're getting Daddy?"

"Can't stop laughing."

"Why don't you tell your cute little lawn guy to bring his wife over? Give her a towel and sponge and tell her to keep turning Daddy like a rotisserie chicken so he doesn't get bed sores. Then go to Santa Fe, you and Gracie."

I hear a swish and imagine Lisa pushing her long thick brown hair off her shoulders. All three of us sisters inherited the same soft packing of chestnut brown hair. Lisa recently clipped the front for bangs, which she calls the biggest worst beauty decision of the decade. I keep mine thick and long and cupped in a ponytail. And Claire, according to Chinese whispers, has shaved her head.

Those Calaway girls. Statuesque and leggy, great babysitters, even Claire, until she turned fourteen and our worlds detonated.

I bread the shrimp and fry them on the stove—what Mrs. Berry's mother would have called Shrimp Nice.

"What does Grandpa eat?" Gracie asks.

"Applesauce maybe?"

"He doesn't have any teeth."

"That's a fact."

"Then I don't have to share my pie."

"Second fact."

She dips her shrimp in ketchup.

"I'll help you, Mama. I mean, with Grandpa. He can watch TV with me."

"That's very obliging of you, Gracie."

"If we lose power in the storm, though, I really think you should take him somewhere." She waves her fork in circles in the air.

Fact three.

Later in the evening, I sit with a book beside Gracie while she does her homework. I want to smooth out the soft ruching of her frown with my fingers, but I keep my hands at my side. My mother used to leave the room if any of us looked on the point of emotion. She was horrified by feelings. She thought feelings, like brown recluse spiders, hid under everyone's floorboards.

We fall asleep to radio—Gracie humming to tunes, me absorbing the death toll of Hurricane Che's landfall in Cuba. It's coming. And Daddy's coming, too.

TUESDAY

8

It seems like just a few hours later that I wake Gracie for school. She gives me a sleepy nod. Her lips are the color of chicory. Her eyes are sunken and her dark eyelashes, long as palm fronds, rest on her cheeks. It almost hurts to see to her guileless beauty, because it's a reminder of my inability to protect her. Certainly I wasn't able to shield her from her father's rages. Now that he's gone, I can't protect her from his absence.

"Is there school today?" Gracie whispers. She is in a place between dreams and day.

"Yes," I say. Don't kill the messenger.

"But the storm."

"It's not here yet."

I make coffee and toast English muffins while flipping through the *Chronicle*. Hurricane season kicks off in June and drills our teeth until November. By now the whole Gulf of Mexico is twitching with anxiety. There are several cornucopia-shaped diagrams in the newspaper projecting Hurricane Che's possible routes through the warm waters. People from Biloxi to Cancun are rooting for the other to take the punch. We must look like a miserable lot to the rest of the country—low-hanging fruit for any storm worth a name. Our FEMA forms pre-filled and just waiting on a date.

Hurricane Che was named back in 2013, the Year of the Snake, when Edward Snowden felt he had no other option than to dump American secrets on the worldwide web, when the Baltimore Ravens won the Superbowl, and "twerk" entered the English language. That was the year Pitti Palazzo sold gorgeous green velveteen A-line coats with gold buttons.

The National Weather Service publishes a list of names

for Atlantic storms six years out, like the Irish, naming babies before they have them, recycling their Cúchulainns and Michaels and Annes for generations of infants to come. Twelve days ago in the tropics, a low-pressure system started to build. It twirled gradually into a spiral of gusty winds and rain, and that was going to be Che—an infant with its name already stenciled in the family album.

Che formed after Bethany, which veered up the Florida coastline in an unhurried expedition of flooding. Bethany came after Hurricane Amos, which tested New Orleans's patched levees, and like a thwarted grump, went on to blow over something else—like Lafayette, Louisiana.

Che formally entered the tropical storm alphabet last Wednesday. It became a hurricane on Saturday and celebrated its promotion on Monday by mowing over Haiti and Cuba, leaving a mud puddle and a landfill behind it. Che is plodding and huge, and there is something indecent about the way it sloshes its weight around the Gulf.

The latest news on Che indicates it is Cat 2 and disorganizing. The storm may zero in on the Yucatan or South Texas. The mayor of Houston suggests we all shelter with a prudent supply of necessities (towels, batteries, water, peanut butter, and ice). Ice is the critical thing. The single most reassuring sound before a tropical storm tracks into your front yard is the cracking and popping of a healthy ice machine. I'm listening to mine now. There's a full tank of gas in my car, and ten boxes of Pop Tarts in the pantry to minister to my anxiety.

I live in a brick house, and for wise or witless it gives me the confidence of the third little pig. This is an old house, built in 1949 on a modest rise of gumbo not far from Buffalo Bayou. My step-grandfather, just back from the war, bought it through the GI Bill. I can't count the number of hurricanes that have pulled the shutters off our windows, sloshed mud under the doors, and knocked over our trees.

People still like to remember Carla, the Cat 4 storm that

pummeled Houston on September 11, 1961 (another 9/11). Old-timers tell stories about the twenty-two-foot storm surge, which washed over Galveston and deposited salt and shrimp on rice farms ten miles inland. A builder in Texas City found a four-foot spiny black iguana from the Yucatan in his driveway. Black iguanas are prized for boots and speed, and this one ran. Hurricane Carla also brought tornadoes—dozens of them. They plucked out trees like tweezers after the rain had loosened their roots.

I remember Hurricane Alberto, not personally, but because I was born on that night in a candlelit ward of Christus St. Joseph's Hospital. Winds had toppled the power lines before the storm ever touched land. The Percocet worked all right at room temperature, and I think they super-sized my mother's dose (for which I will always be grateful), because she recalled this childbirth as the only one she endured without screaming all to hell from the agony. She said the heat that night was so intense that the blood that spilled onto her thighs felt cold. One of the nurses fanned her with a palm frond as the doctor guided me into the world.

"You were all hunched up and skinny," my mother used to say, presenting me with that archival image, affixing to page one of my personal photo album the anti-fanfare of my existence. "The only one didn't try to rip me in two. You never did go looking for trouble." Saying this, she would cast a sideways glance at my sisters. She was our warder, and in the penitentiary paradigm of families, our mother pegged my older sister, Lisa, for a low-security reformatory, and my younger sister, Claire, for solitary confinement. Me, I was the type slated for early parole and then lost in the system.

Our mother carried three babies home from St. Joe's. In those days a woman was left in a darkened room to scream out the first hours of her labor. I'd rather have squatted in a jungle full of snakes than in an antiseptic Catholic institution without a heart.

Maybe that's what I want to tell her in my dreams.

The phone rings as I'm fixing Gracie's English muffin.

"Hey, Julia."

Goosebumps burst across my arms. "Bobby, you're not supposed to be calling me," I say, with as much force as I can muster.

"Don't be frightened," he snorts. "We were married for ten years. We can talk, can't we? That's what normal human beings do."

"There was a court order, Bobby." I try to sound measured, but my pulse thumps in my voice. I survey the kitchen to make sure he's not calling from under the table or behind the laundry door. I'm not scared. What more can he do? I'm mad. Well, I'm a little scared.

"I've said I'm sorry a million times for Christ's sake," Bobby snaps. What's a few sharp slaps between spouses? "For crying out loud. I only wanted to give you the news. I'm flying up to Cambridge for an Old English conference. Harvard invited me—me—because they realized that I stuck honestly to the *Beowulf* text. Heaney thought his poetry should be king. I knew he'd be exposed for the narcissist he is. I thought you'd be happy for me."

"I am."

"You're a liar."

I'm happy he'll be far away. I'm distressed that he has no one else to tell.

"You're happy I'll be gone. You'd probably be happy if I died."

I say nothing.

He adds, and I can hear his provocative grin: "I was thinking I should take Gracie with me, get her out of the hurricane's path."

"You leave Gracie alone. We're fine here."

"Fine?"

"Don't call me again."

"You tried to ruin me. You told them I was dangerous.

Do you know what that word did to me? Do you have any idea how many tribunals I've had to face?"

In court, I'd described life with Bobby as intimate terrorism. Inside the walls of this house, I lived in fear—fear that he might come home angry from Rice, or that some petty event would set him off.

"Leave me alone, Bobby."

"Christ, you're a bitch."

He slams down the phone with such force I think the plastic must have exploded. The whack of receiver into cradle is just too much like the sound of his palm on my face. My arms seize up against my ribs.

The call has left me shaking. A light sweat chills my forehead. I burn my lip on a sip of coffee. Lisa once warned me that divorce never ends. Now, as my heart is battering against my chest, I understand. I stare out at the lawn, parched to the color of wheat, and wonder where Bobby is.

Gracie skips into the kitchen in her school uniform. "Ready," she chirps, still barefoot as a yard dog. "What was all the noise?"

I clasp her in my arms. "I was yelling at your English muffin."

She gives me a narrow glance.

"Gracie, are you frightened about the hurricane?"

"Heck no."

I cast my eyes outside, thinking that I would love to wake up with the certainty of a child.

"What are you looking at?" Gracie asks.

"Squirrels."

"My science teacher says squirrels fall out of trees when they don't have enough potassium."

"Who would have thought?"

Gracie puts a banana in her jumper pocket. "Bananas get gassed," she says, not perturbed. "My science teacher says we're gonna have a great year. We have a new flu from China

and a line of hurricanes stacked up in the Atlantic. Like air-
planes on a runway, she said."

It takes a dedicated scientist to call that great. Gracie hop-
skips toward the back door with one sneaker on and one in
hand. She yanks at the door, and it opens with a tomb's sigh.
Heat and humidity wrap around us like bunting. Houstonians
share a little with the British Raj—we inhabit an uninhabitable environment all starched and buttoned up.

My hands are still shaking as I take the wheel. I don't want
to know where Bobby is. I wish the marriage were buried in
Nevada, in those cement-lined pits where the world's radio-
active waste is stacked in barrels. My deepest fear is that one
day the digital billboard on I 59 will flicker "KIDNAPPED
CHILD," and it will be my Gracie, snatched by her father,
who realizes that the profound satisfaction derived from
terrifying me is unlimited.

As I back the Volvo out of the driveway, two boxes of textile designs and fabric swatches for Pitti Palazzo shift in the
trunk. "M.K. is going to start a family," I tell Gracie.

"If he has children, then he should make children's clothing."

"That's exactly what he's thinking."

"He can ask me for ideas," she says. "I have tons of
ideas." She peels her banana. "What's in the boxes?"

"Winter 2022." To be shelved for another time.

"Too bad. Winter. Dark colors, right, Mama? Gloomy,
gloomy winter. I think orange and pink are beautiful together, don't you?"

"I do."

"If you design children's clothing, will you make pants
and shirts and jumpers and sweaters and coats, too?"

"Everything."

"The whole kit-and-caboodle," Gracie says. "Why don't
you design school uniforms?" She plucks at her own. "I
mean, after."

"That's a nice idea."

"You should make things for little girls. We have fashion mojo."

"You certainly do," I say.

"You should make clothes for hurricanes."

That's an interesting idea: rainwear, heat-wear, and despair-wear. It could be packaged like Russian nesting dolls, one inside the other, and you could pull out the rubber boots first, then the rain hat, then the bourbon.

"What would you recommend?" I ask.

"Pink."

"Wouldn't it be nice if a color, like pink, solved things?"

"It does."

We pass Mr. Lanier's house. He's an eighty-year-old widower, who spends his days routing geckos with a leaf blower. We often see him outside in the ironweed. But this morning, the house is quiet.

"We haven't made Mr. Lanier enchiladas in a while, Mama," Gracie reflects. "Maybe he thinks, that we think, that he should be over his sadness by now."

"I hope not." Mr. Lanier's wife passed away in January from an overdose of painkillers, two years after the death of their son in Afghanistan. Gracie and I have taken a baking dish of enchiladas to his house once a month since then, but I believe we're late.

"After the storm we can bring something by," Gracie says. "When will he be fine again?"

"I don't know. Maybe never." I surely sound as grim as my mother.

"Will we bring casseroles until he dies?"

"It wouldn't be the worst thing." His face, each time we ring his doorbell with a hot dish in our mitts, is so grateful and bewildered.

Gracie muses, "Do you think old Mr. Lanier's geckos *like* flying out of the bushes? Maybe they think, wow, I'm flying? Maybe we shouldn't be feeling sorry for them. Maybe they race back into the bushes for another turn. Do geckos cry?"

"You'll have to ask your science teacher."

"Daddy says only wimps cry."

Bobby. Whatever love I felt for him years ago ran dry, like Spindletop, and now I dread everything about him—Gilgamesh to Grendel.

"I'm not so sure," I say slowly, "that tears are a measure of mettle."

"Metal?"

"Courage."

Gracie frowns. Adults ruin everything. "I'm not a crier," she says.

I pull into the carpool lane.

"Uh-oh," Gracie exclaims. "There's Mrs. Long, the substitute. Maybe one of the teachers has the new Chinese flu! Mrs. Long gives lunch detentions if your shoelaces are untied."

"That seems harsh."

"It's because she's old as dirt. Old people are annoying."

"Gracie, that's not a phrase I—"

"Pooooor Mrs. Long," Gracie toots, rolling her eyes. "She is rather ooooold."

"I'll miss you while you're gone," I say, hugging her young, tiny bones.

Children are resilient, my mother used to cluck, as though we were nothing more than inflatable tenpin clowns with a lead weight in the bottom; we took a punch and bobbed back up.

Gracie looks at me. She has Bobby's eyes, the color of a Texas sky. She can sense I'm scraping zero.

"It'll be okay, Mama. You can finish your drawings on the walls, then I'll help you chalk and pin when I get home. But next time, you should make clothes for little girls."

9

I drive to the supermarket for supplies. The shelves of water, peanut butter, and bread are nearly empty. The fruit bins are low. I buy tiny containers of vanilla pudding and applesauce for my father. Canned soups. At home I lock the kitchen door and set fresh coffee to brew.

The radio foments with news of Hurricane Che. We haven't had a hurricane for a few years, so we're ripe for panic. Katrina scared the hair off Houstonians—mostly a few days afterward, when New Orleans moved here. And when Rita loomed on the Gulf, millions of Houstonians tried to leave, creating the most hellacious evacuation in history. Every highway in Texas became a parking lot. It was so insanely horrible that when the next hurricane pinged our radar, evacuation seemed worse than having your house float to Corpus Christi.

I'm staring idly through the kitchen window when, out of the blue, a massive frond from the Phoenix palm cracks and crashes to the ground outside. A handful of nesting doves flutter up into the air. The heavy impact shivers the house just enough to send the rickety old ironing board, hinged behind the pantry door, crashing down to the floor. I'm thoroughly rattled. My knuckles are white on the lip of the porcelain sink and I think surely Bobby is here inside this house and my heart begins to pound. Have I locked us both in?

There's a second's hush, then *bang!* my heavy iron tumbles impossibly onto the floor. The frayed fabric cord uncoils behind it like a dead prairie snake.

Silence, full and fat. I listen for footsteps, for someone else's breathing, but hear only the burp of the coffee maker.

I stoop to retrieve the iron. It was my mother's iron, a

virtual anvil and her one big rosary bead. It's ten times heavier than modern irons, and when it fell it made a pretty divot in the pine floor.

Six months ago Bobby hit me so hard I fell backward, and my head slammed into a stair tread, and I blacked out. I thought I'd died. It was the sound of my skull on the wood—that *crack* registered in my brain as conclusive. In my last instant of consciousness, I wondered if I'd be with my mother again.

Let me go! she shrieks at me in my dreams. But it's not that simple. I'm made of her. The atoms of my being align in her direction, like cows, nose-to-the-wind. My eyes and lips, my long legs and slender feet, this house, that iron, and even bits of Gracie, are yellow road signs with black arrows pointing to her.

I'm heartbroken about the Phoenix palm because my mother adored that tree. It didn't talk back, it didn't wear mini-skirts, and it never dropped bowls of Frito pie on the floor. But we're in drought this September. Labor Day barbecues have to be registered with the fire department, and the Berrys' impatiens look like zombie fingers clawing up from the soil. Finally, even the fat palm that my mother and father planted on their wedding day is showing signs of stress.

Lisa, Claire, and I saw the famous black-and-white photograph when we raided our parents' wedding album. The palm was the size of a pineapple, with a single green plume erupting from its top like a Mardi Gras hat. There was my mother, stamping all over her white silk train as she dug a hole in the sod for it. She used an old shovel of dented iron, something hammered out in a deer blind. It weighs a ton and leans against the garage wall to this day.

In the photograph, Bisskit is wearing a mother-of-the-bride dress two sizes too large. It has a sweet Peter Pan collar, on which she's pinned a heavy rhinestone brooch that drags the neckline down and exposes her bony sternum. She stands behind my mother like a predatory hawk, a cigarette angled from the corner of her mouth. She has one eyebrow hoisted, maybe wondering what the rules for annulment were in Texas.

And there is Daddy, standing off to the right with a whiskey in his hand and looking like he lost the thread of the whole wedding thing. He's talking to someone outside the camera lens. Those were the days when he had hair.

My mother told us the story a thousand million times while she crusted up our school blouses with starch. She told Daddy, "We can't go on our honeymoon until this tree's in the ground." And he said, "Everyone's standing around with a fistful of rice waiting for us to back out of the damn driveway." And she said, "This palm's a goner if we leave it." Then Daddy's parents (Bisskit called them the McAllen Crackers) went berserk and said, "We didn't drive up from the Valley to watch you dig in the dirt." And Bisskit pointed her flaming cigarette at them and said, "Keep the rice—cook it when you get home." And finally Daddy said, "Well, here's a damn shovel. Go and ruin the day." And my mother did.

My parents' marriage seemed like the union of two plants. They escaped a set of rules that had to do with social awareness and love. He was an English teacher at a fine school, and she could hide her shames behind him. She baked cakes without end for school functions she would never attend, too afraid to be caught out by a conversation she didn't understand. She never spoke of her sister, Loretta, or their childhood in the Pee Dee. She was horrified by our soft fleshy bodies and love-craving souls.

Daddy was a vapor in the house. I remember him settled at the kitchen table each morning, with a cup of coffee and a wedge of pie like a man in a rural restaurant, lost behind the local penny newspaper, reading about people he'd never heard of making fortunes from dead plankton a mile under their feet.

"Bye," we shouted, hoisting our book bags before setting out on foot to school.

"That's nice," he murmured.

"Shoo," our mother said.

My parents never spoke about his workday over the dinner table. He didn't say, "Honey, today I explained to them that Mary, Queen of Scots, received a frosty welcome from her cousin, Elizabeth I." Maybe he found it as boring as everyone else. Maybe at school he just stared out the classroom window at the topiaries of the estate next door, and recited his bit on the do-si-do of European monarchs, the politically advantageous marriages that amounted to inbreeding. He pushed through his Tudor curry until he could coach football at 3:20 every day. Out on the turf, people said, his eyes became bright and he'd do one hundred push-ups and two hundred sit-ups with his team, and shout, "Throw the damn thing!" at his adolescent quarterbacks.

At home, a word cost him. Maybe he opened up in the darkness. Did they whisper at night in bed? Did my mother tell him about the grocer at Jamail's, the fancy food market, who wouldn't sell her half a lettuce? Did she tell him Jamail's made her park in the back, not out front next to the Rolls Royces and Bugattis? And did he make noises of loving indignation? Did he turn to her and say, "Do you know, I think Lisa is growing to look like the second cousin of Prince Albert, of the Saxe-Coburg and Gotha clan, don't you?" And she could have replied, "Imagine!" Then she would have added, "Too bad about her nose."

Daddy got ruffled from time to time about the state of someone's lawn, or the potholes on Westheimer. He admired the Berrys' winter ryegrass, coming up like fur inside the St. Augustine. He was convinced the lumpy asphalt on Kirby Drive was ruining his Buick's shocks. He used to walk through the house with his eyes fixed on the floorboards, making little "huh!" noises about the price of crap lumber from cousin Roy in Texarkana. I was allowed to kneel with

Daddy as he scrutinized the living room floor. He'd push his glasses up onto his head and peer at the oak slats like there was more than met the eye. He'd point to dings in the wood and lesser grain patterns, and he once muttered, "Cracker!" and I knew it was his cousin Roy, and I grew up relishing my own contempt for Roy, because it was the only thing I shared with Daddy. My kneeling on the floor and staring at crappy quartersawn oak—for Daddy, that was about as intimate as an Indian princess campout.

He never asked me about school or boyfriends or clothes. If I sewed him a shirt or tie, he wore it. When he walked by me at the sewing machine, he would pat me on the head like I was a banana bread and he was checking my doneness.

Did he pat Claire on her head before he thrust himself inside her?

10

If immortality is being remembered, my mother will live on for a very long time. The grocer from Jamail's says he'll never forget her. She was the woman that asked him to shuck a crate of corn until she found ten cobs to her satisfaction. The Indian man at the Shell on the corner of Kirby and Holcombe remembers her because she insisted he pump her gas even after the self-serve islands went in (she called him a Bunko artist). And the toothless waitress at Captain Benny's said no one else used to insist on extra shrimp in the gumbo, and no one used to steal Saltine packets like my mother.

Maybe Daddy still remembers his wife in a pocket of brain cells. Maybe he remembers her as a young girl, perfect and slim and convinced that she was brighter than Einstein in a very non-bookish way. Gosh, how Lisa and I used to stare at those wedding photographs—the white silk train, pooling like liquefied pearl all around my mother's feet, Daddy with more hair than a Wookie. There was one photograph of the two of them under the white rose arbor at Hermann Park—a public space, no charge—and she already looked determined, her eyes full of defiance, as if she knew damn well why men asked girls to marry and she was going to keep her thighs shut tight as a freezer lid. Daddy stood beside her as though someone asked him to save a place in line. His hands were down at his sides and his expression suggested that playing bench all four years at Columbia was still on his mind, and maybe this wedding thing was just one more incomplete pass.

Bisskit said my mother could have had her pick of the male litter if she just brushed her teeth and kept her mouth shut. Bisskit was like that, always telling you to sit down and stand up at the same time. She was rough on her other daughter, Aunt Loretta, with her bum leg and prosthetic shoes. Bisskit said the gimpy leg precluded marriage to anyone but Jesus H. Christ, and she shipped Loretta off to join the Dominicans. The Dominicans promptly put Loretta on a freighter and mailed her to Guam. She died many years later from a tropical fever. I remember seeing Aunt Loretta's letters ("I simply cannot abide coconut milk...") and the frail Christmas ornaments she sometimes sent back to Texas. The ornaments were made of corn tassels and rice hulls, with seashells glued on. Loretta wrote in pale script, on paper bearing the address of a convent in Los Angeles, and I know my mother wrote back because in her letters Loretta chided my mother about her poor spelling.

My mother was not put on a boat. She was marked out as the money gin for Bisskit's retirement. She worked in the coffee shop counter at the Shamrock Hotel. The Shamrock was Houston's epicenter for glamour, stars, and scandals. One thousand one hundred rooms. A garage for 1,000 cars. Multimillionaires waterskied across its world's largest outdoor swimming pool. Bellhops wore emerald green, and the coffee shop girls wore Veronese green dresses with lime-green aprons. My mother, statuesque and beautiful, must have raked in the stares of men. She told us all of Hollywood proposed to her over that coffee counter. Our mother turned down Jimmy Stewart, Cary Grant, Spencer Tracy, Gregory Peck, and Marlon Brando.

"Why didn't you say yes?" Lisa used to agonize. "I would've loved having Cary Grant as a father."

"If you're thinking you wouldn't've had that nose, you might be right," my mother said.

I have no idea what transpired at that Shamrock coffee counter. It's not easy to imagine my mother smiling at strangers under any circumstances. She probably eyed them over her order pad like a policeman writing out a ticket. Toasted, eh? An extra egg, huh?

Claire, when she was little, loved the stories linking our mother to movie stars. But after The Mess and her in-house demolition, she took pins to every balloon our mother tried to inflate. Claire became our own voodoo priestess. She'd ask what Gregory Peck took in his coffee.

"You think I'm lying, do you?" our mother snapped.

Claire would lift her eyebrows into an expression that said, *Damn right I do*.

"Gregory Peck and Walter Hobbs both took cream and sugar."

Claire would rise from the table and roll her eyes. "Who gives a fuck?"

And then all hell would break loose. It seems like yesterday. The hollering back and forth across the kitchen, then up and down the stairs. I would slip out the back door and get on my fat-tired bike and pedal until all I heard was the blood pounding in my ears.

Ultimately our mother left the Shamrock under circumstances that never made it into her ironing stories. She took a job waitressing at an eatery on Westheimer and Bammel. It was called the Sunshine Shop, and it served kolaches in the morning and gumbo at noon. One day, up to the counter strolled the forgotten McAllen high school football star, who warmed the bench at Columbia for four years. He was the English history teacher at St. John's School, two blocks away. I imagine Bisskit pointed her flaming cigarette at Daddy and nodded once, like the deal was done.

There were no childhood photos of my mother. There were no stories about her hobbies or school plays or nightmares. There had been no one available to her but Loretta, whose club foot marked her for the culling pen.

Our mother grew into a creature of distrust and institutionalized terror. As children we observed her bone-deep fear of cracks in the sidewalk. We saw her pour boiling water on fire ant mounds. We took in her threats and warnings, which became the only kind of love we knew. She cooked our meals until the ingredients laminated, bleached our blouses, and pressed our bras. She nosed the tip of her iron into the last corner of the tiniest stitch, as though every cotton thread were capable of rebellion and in need of violent suppression.

She raised us to believe the world was a den of thieves, who would serve us fried nutria as soon as steak. Our only hope was to marry an Abilene oilman and tip everybody royally at Christmas.

"You marry or you stay invisible," my mother said. We were just three mud pies she had to slap into marriage shape, in return for which (and there was an implicit ledger), down the road, we would install her in a nice nursing home, maybe a little early even, one with soft beds and working televisions and painkillers and a ladder to heaven not made of Cousin Roy's cheap lumber.

Marriage meant insulation from a society of miscreants and crooks. And yet, as it happened, the terror was inside our house, not beyond.

11

The parched grass smells like dust. I drag over the hose and set it to drip on the Phoenix palm. In a few days, that wretched tree will have something like Lake McQueenie thrown on top of it. By that time, the clay-laden ground will have cooked to a porcelain crust, and all the water will sheet into the streets and flood the city. A severe drought upended by a monster hurricane.

I tow the fallen frond to the curb. It's awkward but not too heavy, already drained of its life force. I don't have a clue what Daddy weighs. Will I be able to scoop him from his bed and sit him on the couch during the day? Is it true that people thrust into crisis situations are able to lift amazing burdens—tree trunks, cars? Fathers?

At the end of the driveway I see Jesús, my lawn guy. He's bagging brown, crispy oak leaves with that old iron shovel from our garage. Jesús is just a few inches taller than Gracie, reminding me how short all those murderous Mayans were, herding virgins up the tiny steps of Chichén Itzá to where the hatchets hung. The Mayans left stone reliefs of squat, square, flat-faced people with noses that dominated their somber faces, and five thousand years later, one is raking my leaves.

Bobby used to call Jesús the Burrito. "How did we end up with the big Burrito?" he used to complain.

After years of handing Jesús cash on Fridays, I still don't know his last name. After years of wondering why he won't deadhead the cone flowers, I'm thinking maybe I should hand him a pair of reading glasses.

"*Hola,*" I say, smiling.

"*¿Qué tal, Señora?*"

Jesús is from Guatemala. He used to work in a plant nursery just outside Antigua, growing carnations and geraniums for export. When he was a boy, paramilitary troops burst out of the forest and strafed the nursery. Jesús hid in a hole from which a poinsettia bush had just been excavated. He inched a shipping pallet over the gap and closed his eyes while splinters of wood rained into his skin.

One day I bought a dozen flats of begonias to busy Jesús. He brought his whole familia to admire and plant the flowers. They packed picnic coolers, a portable radio, and a thermos of Hi-C fruit punch. But it's expensive to keep Jesús in begonias so usually he spends the days raking seven leaves back and forth across my lawn. Oak leaves are tough little disks, like pressed pennies, and hard to corral. He rakes with the same doting patience a hairdresser shows to a nice head of hair. I have watched him pick up a single dead leaf and frown contemplatively, like a Sandanista considering a hostage trade. Then he sets the leaf back down on the grass and rakes it.

Once Bobby told Jesús to stop bagging the leaves and to make a compost pile instead. Bobby, to be fair, imagined a steaming, wormy pile of fertile humus that would make Al Gore weep. Jesús nodded thoughtfully at Bobby's unintelligible Spanglish, then Bobby left for work and Jesús bagged the leaves.

Jesús grew up in the kind of poverty that made the whole earth into a pungent, rotting compost pile. Recreating that sepsis in clean, paved, lit, plumbed, Walmart-filled Houston is a sin.

Once I suggested to Jesús that he keep a thin layer of leaves over the soil to preserve the cool and dew. We conferred about the brutal Texas sun and the parching of our soil, which is commonly called gumbo, and which looks exactly like grey peanut butter. I thought Jesús and I had a meeting of the minds, lots of smiles, *entiendo, entiendo*, and the next day the garden beds were scraped clean and my leaves were bagged and stacked curbside to be hauled up to the Humble landfill, which is the size of Bolivia (if my mother ironed it flat).

I can't fire Jesús, although there is virtually nothing for him to do. He came with the house. When we arrived, there was a receipt taped to the kitchen door. The box marked THINGS ARE FINE was checked, and the bottom was signed: JESÚS.

I've kept that piece of paper. And I've kept Jesús.

Lately Jesús has been watering my grass into florescence, which is a screaming felony during this drought. Mrs. Blanton, President of the River Oaks Garden Club, is going to call ICE if it looks any more lush over here. She can't understand why her $125,000 irrigation system doesn't keep pace with Jesús. "Your man," she calls him. "What exactly does your man do?" she asks, glaring at my tiny slip of emerald lawn.

This morning Jesús seems distressed. "El Señor…" Jesús says to me. He's referring to Bobby.

"No más," I say.

Jesús frowns. "Pero…Quiero decir" He points toward the house.

Once I might have thought Jesús would have noticed that Bobby, his car, and his irrational hollering had disappeared.

"Espera," I say. Hold on.

I reach into my wallet and pay him for the week. With the storm coming, he can make extra money helping homeowners nail plywood sheets over their windows. I hand him all my twenties and remind him not to go fishing on Friday. Jesús loves to drive onto the sand at Surfside and fish for crappies all day long. Crappies stampede around the Gulf like wild herds of water bison.

I head back into the house. A vexed Jesús is still leaning on his rake, nodding his head as though re-evaluating Pythagoras.

12

My parents had their worst fights about hurricanes. Daddy had his McAllen Plan, which was to ride it out. My mother had her Pee Dee Plan, which was early evacuation with a caveat about never coming back. Every time a tropical storm started curling its tail in the Gulf, she threatened to load the mattresses on top of the station wagon and drive to Lubbock. It wasn't the storm that scared my mother most, but the aftermath—the fans motionless, the refrigerator warm, the lights off, the oven unresponsive, and the iron cold.

"I'm leaving!" my mother screamed hysterically.

Daddy's eyebrows wouldn't even lift. Daddy's eyebrows never lifted, even before The Mess. English history had numbed his emotions. All those inbred faces frozen in oil in Grimsthorpe Castle had reached out and pre-embalmed him. He sat in the living room while my mother shrieked around the house, and he would read his newspaper. Daddy could read the daily newspaper for hours.

Sometimes my mother ordered us to help carry laundry baskets full of her clean, pressed clothing out to the car. Then we'd go upstairs and watch television with the enthusiasm of those knowing the last hours of electricity were upon us. We didn't witness Part II, where she burst into sloppy tears halfway down the driveway. In all her years of marriage, she'd never driven past Katy without my father. She had no credit cards, no idea of where to go—where was Lubbock, really, anyway? And how on earth did so much of Mexico get north of Houston on the damn map? She would crawl back into the house with the resignation of the condemned, close the door to her bedroom and run a last hot bath. Lisa, Claire, and I brought her clothes back upstairs, dragged the mattress back inside, whispered to Daddy, "She's back."

And he would say, "How's your mother?"

"Okay."

"That's good."

My mother gave some thought to those she intended to leave behind. She taped an emergency list of necessary items on the refrigerator door.

FOOD, she wrote.
Canned food
Canned juises
Peanut butter and honey
Crackers

RED CROSS
Cotton
Iodine
Balfer's snake bite kit
Bandages
Petroleum jelly
Gauze and tape
Antiseptic
Fever-reader
Soap
Hydrogen perox-cide
Asprin

She picked the right church. The Catholics never set their sights on scholars.

Finally the hurricane would arrive. We would tiptoe downstairs into the kitchen while wind and rain howled from the four corners of the earth, and there she'd be in the dimness, staring at her cold iron with holy terror, fingering the dangling cord as though it had been ripped from life's own womb.

Up in my studio, I hear on the radio that Hurricane Che has rolled over Haiti like a farm combine, churning the country into silage. You can say all you want about the fifty miles between Houston and Galveston, but Che seems ready to minimize the margin of safety.

I unpin the neckline of a shift draped on one of my dress forms, and pry open the darts. I love the forgiving nature of fabric, its capacity to hide faults. You can cut and sew and rip and it never bleeds. Every hemline, every dart, every pleat, every seam is subject to replacement. I pinch and poke the fabric on my dress forms relentlessly, looking for a fresh silhouette. Fabric is the one thing in life I can control.

I commandeered this unfinished attic for my studio when Bobby and I moved to Houston. I swept up decades of dead flies, weightless as rice hulls, and vacuumed between the floorboards. There were full inch gaps between the withered pine planks. The vacuum sucked up years of dehydrated little bodies—powder-post beetles, sugar ants, flies, termites, roaches, moths, love bugs. They clattered up the hose like sand. My mother used to rage about the attic flooring.

"Those weren't our bugs," she complained, ironing someone's collar into a dollar bill. "They came with the pine boards. Gospel truth. From Texarkana, some cousin of your daddy had a sawmill. Roy, it was. He said your daddy wasted a perfectly good degree from Co-lum-bi-a and who the hell cared what the lard-ass English ever did?"

The very memory would kindle my mother's ire.

"Was one day at the sawmill that a brown recluse bit him—bit Roy in the stomach and laid its eggs in there. By the time Roy went to the doctor, he was a goner. The funeral parlor scooped out the egg sack before they cremated Roy. Don't ask me why. And one week later Roy's wife got poked in the eye by a passer's umbrella and died of a brain hemorrhage. You want excitement? Try Texarkana."

Our lives were infected by her fear. We lived in constant

terror of viruses, bugs, rabid strays, botulism in our canned beans, and trichinosis in our pork. Brown recluse spiders scared us half to death. It was always, "Don't step there! Brown recluses love under-porches." "Better not put your foot in that boot without shaking it!" "Don't you know what a brown recluse can do to a person? Might as well plan your casket attire."

13

I measure and photograph the images on my studio walls. I drape and pin five dress forms in Indian silk and fine cotton, using three new color variations. Resort colors. Bright and sunny. It's the beginning of an idea. M.K. will modify the palette. I itemize the thread numbers, button sizes, ribbon specs, and zipper charms, and email everything to Leona.

My alarm beeps. It's time to pick Gracie up from school.

If I complained about walking to and from school, my mother advised me how she trekked halfway across the Albemarle to school every day, even during thunderous storms, along mud roads with thick wood planks tossed across them. When the family moved to Texas, it was the same all over again, but worse. She leapt over alligators and water moccasins in the drainage ditches, shook scorpions and warty toads from her rubber boots.

Once that troublemaker boy, Jeffers Creskie, tried to skip school by jumping out a classroom window, but he slipped on the wet tiles and landed in a sago palm, and lay wrapped in bandages in a hospital bed until he died three weeks later from infection. Our mother told us about Jeffers again and again. He was one of her favorite ironing stories. Sometimes he slipped off the porch roof, its tar paper slick as ice in the bad weather. Sometimes he landed on the black thorns of a devil palm. But no matter the details, in the end he was gone. People just disappeared in her childhood. People died. Children died. Maybe that's why she ironed like an addict. To smooth out what bumps she could.

It's one hundred degrees outside. The pavement sends up quivering plumes of air. I see old Mr. Lanier blowing geckos into the air. He's wearing safety goggles and cushioned ear protectors, and he's strapped the leaf blower to his back. An orange extension cord snakes back to his house. Tiny lizards are springing out of the ironweed like skeet clays.

I stop and he walks slowly over to my car.

"You staying?" he asks.

"I'll be here with Gracie."

"I'm going to ride it out in Columbus," he says. "Got a cousin."

"That's a good idea."

"I'm putting the house on the market," he says. "Start fresh somewhere else. You should, too. Get rid of that professor. He's a bad penny."

"I—" I say, thinking to bring him up to date. But not now. "I'll be sad to see you leave."

"Too many memories. They won't let me go."

In the school parking lot, the weight of what's about to happen crashes through my spirits like a chunk of meteorite. A tear leaks down my cheek. Everyone else is worrying about the hurricane, and I have visions of turning my house into a nursing home—white beds and boiled sheets and disinfectant smells.

In the old days, you always took in your dying relatives, and they had the decency not to last long. Bisskit told us about a great-aunt from South Carolina who lay dying in the dining room one year. The woman had traveled down to Houston from the Albemarle to recuperate from postpartum fever, the result of a stillborn baby. She arrived half-dead, Grandma said, the color of cooked hake, and with an unopened bottle of medicinal whiskey in her bag. It didn't take much in those days. A bite, a scratch, a bone-deep grief, and you could practically hear the bells tolling.

Bisskit dragged a mattress downstairs to accommodate this poor woman, who walked through the door with her last ounce of Could and then collapsed onto the floor. The dining room wasn't the worst place. The french doors let soft northern light in through the gauzy curtains. My mother was a little girl. She told me the house smelled of urine, and she and Loretta took their plates outside to eat. Charlotta? Georgina? The age-old story of a mother and baby dying around childbirth. When I was young, I would wander into the dining room and lie on the floor, pretending I was the ill-starred, fading relative. Those self-same curtains still hang along the french doors. They used to be as rough as cheese-cloth. Maybe they were nothing more than strips of tobacco netting. Too many trips through the washing machine later, they're as thin as gold leaf.

I blot the tears on my sleeve and smack off the radio with my elbow just as I get the news: the storm trajectory has shifted northward, making a beeline toward Houston. The whole Yucatán is probably dancing in the streets. Daddy will be discharged at my front door tomorrow like a new puppy, and then Hurricane Che is going to pulverize our physical world.

I park directly in front of the sign that reads Do Not Leave Valuables In Your Car and shove my bag under the seat and head into the school. I join a thickening trickle of mothers in the atrium. There are eight to ten of us who reg-ularly avoid the drive-thru pick-up and walk into the building to meet our children. Statistically, four of us will divorce, one of us will develop breast cancer, and three of our children are already taking Ritalin. I wonder if anyone else is taking in a dying relative.

"Are you leaving tonight?"

"Do you have batteries?"

"Will you be staying with relatives?"

"How did you find a hotel?"

From a few feet away, we probably sound like a covey of doves. During the school year, I can rely on these moms for critical information: which child (needing FBI protection) introduced the lice; whether a test counts for 12.5 percent or 13 percent of the final grade; whose divorce is imminent.

When it comes to national news, such as who qualifies as a counter-insurgent, their interpretations are less firm to the touch.

Kelly, a stay-at-home mother with one of those nebulous degrees in marketing everything, says, "Chinese people believe hurricanes are sent by Buddha to punish us."

"Punish us for what?"

"For not living in the moment. We run after ignorant desires."

I stand next to MaryJane, doyenne of our mother-scrum. MaryJane is my friend, the kind of friend who is loyal and loving, and mercurial and sometimes mean, too.

"Baloney," MaryJane says. "And by the way, hurricanes form from African winds. Not to trouble you with science or anything."

MaryJane is a bona fide Houston socialite, a cousin of both a Weingarten and a Sakowitz. MaryJane can afford Pitti Palazzo fashions. She could buy Pitti's whole fall line in one fell swoop, but she prefers bling to Italian elegance, because bling, in Houston, is kind of everything.

Tomorrow, MaryJane is evacuating ahead of the hurricane. She and her daughter, Emma, are boarding a plane to Paris.

"Do you think this is too much?" she asks me, pointing to a Cartier tiger-under-palm-tree brooch nearly invisible on a silk Hermes blouse. "I'm thinking of wearing it on the plane."

"It's perfect," I say.

She looks hard into my eyes and growls, "I'll take it off."

"No! Don't." I laugh, putting an arm around her. "It's Houston, MaryJane. If you lived in New York, it would be black, black, black and big diamonds. And if you lived in New York, you wouldn't have to dress for hurricane evacuation anyway. Well, rarely."

"How come you never evacuate?"

"I'm not scared enough."

"Julia, you're scared of everything."

I shrug. This is just the kind of banter designed to slip me quickly and efficiently into my coffin.

"I read the most interesting article," says another mother. "It said there's proof that Jesus had a dog."

I feel MaryJane tense again, ready to spring.

Kelly considers the issue. "I'd figure Jesus for a King Charles spaniel."

MaryJane closes her eyes and inhales Pranayamas, her nostrils flaring. After a few breaths she turns to tell me about her husband, Mickey's, newest project—a 38,000 square foot restaurant.

"Gold burlap on the walls?" I asked, giggling.

"You were away from Houston too long," MaryJane says. "You've forgotten how to think big."

A sour evangelical woman named Therese says, "Here's our economy going to hell in a handbasket, and Mickey has to build some new shrine to foodies."

"Isn't that a good thing?" I ask. "A sign of hope and commerce?"

"It's a sign," Therese says, "that he's going to take a few banks down with him."

There's a chilly pause in our group. Then someone chirps, "So, are they going to open the contraflow lanes?" and the conversation bubbles back into life.

"You're not going to evacuate, Julia?" Therese says. "Don't you worry about Gracie?"

"No, never," MaryJane snorts derisively. "Look, Therese, even the mayor said to stay and hunker down."

Therese raises her eyebrows. "At the last parent education meeting, they said young girls were particularly prone to anxiety attacks."

"I'll tell you who's prone to anxiety attacks," MaryJane says. "Me. Know what? Life goes on."

"I gather your life is going to Paris," Therese says.

"Yes," MaryJane replies. "Paris, France. I'll look into parent ed there. *Bonne idée.*"

The first few children are coming downstairs from the classrooms. Gracie is among them. She comes skipping into view with a big, bright, cherry-red stain down the front of her plaid jumper. From fifty feet, I can tell it is irremediable.

"Uh-oh," says Therese with grim satisfaction.

MaryJane is used to cameras and red carpets and bald envy. "Therese," she says. "Gracie is the only girl on earth that looks cuter than usual with a big red stain on her jumper." She swings her hip affectionately into mine. "I'm going to go home and toss red wine at myself."

Gracie flings her arms around MaryJane.

"Have a wonderful trip," I say to MaryJane.

"Come with us," she says.

"I can't." I see a trace of hurt in her expression. Her daughter, Emma, is pulling on her arm. I'm too embarrassed to tell MaryJane about Daddy.

Gracie says, "I love hurricanes. You should see what we get up to. Right, Mama?"

"I am so jealous," MaryJane says, squeezing her.

Gracie brims with an itemization of the day's events as we drive home. She iterates, without pause, the full cherry-red (slushy) story, in great detail, the unfairness of a quiz, the amazing shoelaces of a friend. It's like a river of sweet words that carries my worries away.

14

At home, I quickly examine Gracie's jumper to see whether it belongs in the laundry or the trash. Trash. Gracie flies from the kitchen.

"My bladder's bursting!" Gracie screams. "What stinks? Are we having the house painted?"

A terrible latex smell permeates the house. Could we possibly have a gas or oil leak just before the storm?

Nose first, I poke through the downstairs rooms to see if anything is the obvious source of the odor. A vent, a fireplace? Nothing.

My eyes sting. I check the laundry room to see if bleach spilled. I look under the sink for something of chemical terrible-ness. The smell is familiar but huge in its proportions.

I set out some cut-up watermelon for Gracie and open the back door for fresh air. Heavy heat muscles in like a slob.

"What smells so terrible? Oh, watermelon! Yay!"

"What was lunch today?" I ask her. I open the kitchen window too. More wet heat hulks into the room.

"Chicken fingers."

"Good?"

"Cold. You can't point to the ones you want. I have Fear of Lunch Ladies," Gracie cries out (she makes some death-rattle noise). I have difficulty imagining her cowed.

"What smells so bad?" she asks again.

"I don't know." We both sniff thoughtfully. The open window has helped.

I put my nose to the stairway. There is a distinct paint odor. Sometimes when I work with oil crayons, my nose becomes inured to the scent. But this is more industrial.

"How is the new teacher?" I ask.

"We're doing the human body."

"Interesting?"

"Do you have to have hair?"

"Afraid so."

"Daddy is totally overgrown."

"What do you mean?" I ask. Bile creeps into my mouth.

"Doesn't matter," Gracie announces. She's said something incendiary and knows it. Suddenly her hands leap up to her face in alarm. "Seed!" She runs to the trashcan and vomits up a half-chewed slurry of pink watermelon. Then she pants with great melodrama.

"It's only a seed," I say. My molars are conjoined. Daddy is overgrown?

"Can't you buy the seedless ones?" She reviews the rest of the watermelon chunks with antipathy and stuffs the bowl back into the refrigerator.

"It was a seedless watermelon, Gracie." She knows that.

"I've had a long day," she sighs, heading up to her room. "School was annoying." Clomp, clomp. "The smell is worse up here. Can we open the windows?"

I head upstairs, and the odor is indeed worse. I open all the windows. Gracie lies on the floor of her room. Her feet are up on a chair and she's staring at a mobile I made for her years ago. I'd bought a bag of jacquard scraps from Universal Fabric and sewn six-inch clouds, and from each I hung balls of bluebonnet blue rain. Then I'd embroidered the clouds with sparkly beads. Then, because once I get going…I'd sewn and stuffed little purple birds flying through the rain. Something comes over me when I have a threaded needle and a bit of cloth.

The odor peaks as I climb to the attic. Horrible and industrial. I flick on the studio fluorescents. And scream. I scream so loudly I choke.

My drawings are gone. The swing dress and its summery coat, the crepe skirt with oversized mother-of-pearl buttons, the cap shoulder dress with the silk bow, the tie-waist blouses with Japanese gimp, the tabbed trousers—they are all lost under buckets and buckets of black latex house paint. My dress forms are dripping, glossy, sticky, ruined, hellish, headless black figures. The walls are splashed and splattered in black. Baskets of fabric are glistening black tubs. The worktables are drenched, dripping, and destroyed. I fling open the attic windows and drop to my knees.

All things heal and hair over. That's what Bisskit used to say. A neat marriage of stoicism and bitterness.

I don't hear the phone ring. Misery resounds in my ears like a chorus of cicadas. Through underwater eyes, I see Gracie in the doorway with the handset. She stares at the walls. Her small mouth—her lips are a pale pink-violet—drops helplessly open. I hear Lisa's disembodied voice through the jelly of my consciousness.

Gracie offers me the handset.

"Julia," Lisa says. "Didn't you get my message?"

"Your what?" My cellphone. Vaguely I remember putting my handbag under the car seat at school.

"I left you a message," Lisa says. "I have bad news. Bobby was by the house this afternoon."

I drink down a slug of sloppy tears. "Wait. How do you know?"

"Someone saw him and called me."

"Oh, Lisa," I cry. I tell her about the walls.

Lisa bellows in outrage. "I'm going to call your lawyer and the judge," she says. "I'm going to hang Bobby's nuts for sale in Krogers. Stay on the line, Julia."

I stare at the black paint, thick and splashy, glossy wet and gooey, pooling in places on the floor. It's like crude oil. The stench is sickening. Gracie creeps into my lap and pulls my arms around her. She's not defending her father right now. She's frightened. Poor Gracie, to see the madness of her daddy. How will I protect us from Bobby, who has waded off reality's shores into some delusional sea?

"What is Aunt Lisa saying?" she whispers. She pinches her nose shut.

"I'm on hold."

That gets a sweet giggle. Gracie loves hearing about Aunt Lisa's oversized life. On Lisa's end, clicks and pings and then her beloved voice yelling at someone else.

"I'll ask her," Lisa says to whomever. Then, "Julia, I've got your big bad lawyer on line three. Did you call the police?"

"Not yet. I only just came up here when you called."

"No," Lisa says to my lawyer, Trey Coombs. "She just discovered it. Tell her not to touch anything? Coombs, it's buckets of black paint. What the hell would she want to touch?"

I imagine Lisa's desk with its six phones and three computer screens. I look at my two worktables. My fabric, my pins and pin cushions, my beautiful gimps are smothered and lost and ruined.

A little voice in my other ear whispers, "I'm going to get more watermelon now." I give Gracie a squeeze and she leaps from my lap like a finch from the feeder.

Lisa says, "Julia, he needs to know if the house was locked."

"I think so."

"Julia. Really? You don't lock the fucking door?"

"Don't yell at me, Lisa."

"This is Bobby on the loose. You've got to protect yourself."

"I can't," I say. I burst into new bubbly tears.

"Oh dear," Lisa sighs. "Coombs, I'm putting you on hold. Move one inch from your phone and I'll donate your fees to an Indian reservation. Julia? You there?"

"I keep thinking about Claire," I say.

"Wow. This is so not about Claire."

"It's about violence. I feel like I'm repeating something awful."

"Double wow. You're scaring me a little, Julia. First I'll call the police, and then I'm going to find you a psychiatrist."

"I feel like it should have been me," I whisper. "I was no one."

As soon as I left for Parsons, my mother ironed my room with vinyl wallpaper, greasing my exit from the house, hoping I would be wooed and carted off by a door-to-door salesman, who would staple his business card to a Christmas note once a year.

"Don't you like it?" she'd asked. "Cleans with a damp sponge."

It was kelly green with silver squares—wallpaper from the box in between CLEARANCE and DUMPSTER.

I was no one.

"Stay with me, Julia," Lisa says.

"I wanted to protect Claire. And I couldn't."

"You need to protect Gracie."

"Why didn't our mother help us?"

Lisa is silent a moment. "She didn't know how. Remember the dead bolts on our doors? It was all she could do."

We sit quietly on the line. Then Lisa says, "Hold on, Julia." She presses a button. "Coombs?" But her voice is tired now. "Listen to me. I don't give a rat's ass if she should have mined the front sidewalk. We're talking trespass and vandalism. Premeditated. He took advantage of her. He must have been watching the house because he did it when she went to pick up Gracie."

I suddenly remember Jesús (mine) mentioning El Señor. And then Mrs. Blanton, who said Bobby looked well. Why didn't it click? He'd been lurking around the house. Was it he that left the garage doors open? What else had I missed?

Lisa argues with Coombs. I can only register bits. "Not to make housekeeping suggestions…incapable of protecting herself. I hired you…" She hangs up on Coombs with a bang.

"Sigma-Pi jerk," Lisa grumbles. "Julia. Bobby is going to prison. You've atoned enough, okay? No one knew about Daddy. No one."

My mind is tumbling. I am suddenly so tired that I can feel

the skin on my face tug down. I hear Lisa saying something about revenge.

My mother knew a thing or two about revenge. Revenge made her feel all *Domini, Domini, Domini*. She could have been God's bounty hunter.

Originally the welcome committee at St. Vincent's tried to include her in churchy things, Good Samaritan outings, the flower guild; they asked her to bake pound cakes for Easter receptions, coffee cakes for Christmas receptions, and cupcakes for the christening receptions, but eventually those phone calls tapered off. My mother didn't seize on Catholicism for company, and she wasn't looking to share recipes. She was looking for hope. She bought a silver WWJD bracelet and some Bakelite worry beads. She did her real praying at home, in private, maybe so that no one would see how close to begging it was for her.

Our mother admired the whole eye-for-an-eye business. It is fixed in my memory, the image of her behind her ironing board, assigning blame for the last transgression while we ate breakfast. This constituted homeschooling.

"Was a fella that cut in front of me at Jamail's bread counter," she'd begin, eyes wide with the horror of it, one eyebrow hiked up to let you know this incident, like all of them, was a morality tale fit for the history books. Jamail's supermarket was grocer to the millionaires. Mrs. Jamail, who oversaw the fresh produce, wore a mink coat into the cooler. We only ever went there to buy a loaf of fresh bread or a vegetable, something that didn't break the bank, something that allowed us to include ourselves in the Jamail's magic and the Jamail's air-conditioning.

"Fella had a straw hat on with a brim as wide as a car tire," our mother recalled. "Only a cracker wears his hat indoors," she added, craning over the ironing board, her eyes sparkling dark and fiery, pressing Daddy's shirt cuffs into paper. "That brim was so wide he made out as not seeing me. Well, this fella took to ordering one of everything, a monkey bread fresh from the back, one of them thumb-pressed jam cookies, one of the chocolate wafers, one of the strawberry tarts, no-not-that-one-this-one. I said, 'Sir,' (she accosted him; we gasped!) 'may I remind you that there are other people walking this earth besides you, and three of them are waiting in this line?'"

Lisa, Claire, and I nearly fainted. Did the man apologize on his knees? Did he call the police?

Our mother straightened up in saintly indignation. She'd tell us she'd forgiven the offender in her soul. Poor bastard.

I close the windows of the attic studio. Air conditioning will dry the paint and suck up the fumes better than Mother Nature. Pitti Palazzo got the JPEGs. In their records are the inventory of my swatches and gimp. It can all be recreated.

15

The first creatures to evacuate from oncoming storms are the roaches. They evacuate from outside to inside, from my garage to my kitchen. In Houston we have American roaches, tree roaches, and wood roaches—all rotten fliers and nearly blind, all big enough to make you shriek.

Gracie peruses a teen magazine while eating her melon. She copies the dresses she likes onto a piece of paper. She hasn't spotted the tree roach on his back under the stove. Gracie could out-scream a Delta banshee. The roach is wiggling his limbs helplessly. He's over two inches long. I sidle toward the paper towels.

"I see him," Gracie says without looking up.

New world order.

The doorbell rings.

Through the thick-cut glass I see Enrique, our dyslexic mailman, in pith helmet and blue post-office-issue button-down. He was assigned to our route after Miss Martha retired. Poor Miss Martha. My mother said that only loose women walked a mail route. She was sure Miss Martha stopped in each male household and swapped liberties for cash. So Miss Martha never got a Christmas tip from our house, and for some reason our mail always arrived wet, practically hosed down, and we had to lay each piece out on the floor to dry.

Today Enrique is holding a fat envelope that has a 25 percent likelihood of being mine.

"I have a package," he calls through the glass. At fifty-something, his skin is leathery and brown. Liver spots mottle his skin, and he seems to have a new tattoo, making me wonder how much ink a body can drink before it flops over.

Before delivering mail, Enrique worked as a fry cook for the military. He retired with full benefits, drifted, got bored, took the Postal Worker test, flunked, and got the job. He says traipsing around Houston on 100-degree days is a garden party compared to feeding the chow line in Iraq.

I open the door and Enrique's grin stretches into a surprised O. "Whew! Somebody's painting, eh?" He fans away the paint odor with my mail.

"Something like that," I say.

"Sign right here." Enrique hands me a clipboard and a moist pen. "I love sweating. Better than listening to my kidneys wither in Sadr City." He hoists his blue shirt and treats me to a gravity-stricken abdomen.

I sign for the package.

"Thank God that last hurricane didn't find us," Enrique says. "I hear the new one, Che, is gonna blast us." Enrique jabs a right hook into the air, which anyone superstitious would read as a warning to Beaumont. "I'll have to deliver your mail in fishing waders next week." His joke makes him delirious with laughter. "God bless," he sighs.

I thank him and watch him wander down the walk. Those charismatic faiths win in the happiness department. I open the package.

It's a book. By Bobby. *Grendel, the Injured Son.*

I first met Bobby during my scholarship years at Parsons in Manhattan. Precisely, on a bench at Washington Square Park. I was sketching outfits and he was eating a hotdog with sauerkraut. There were two of us on the bench, and he said, "Nietzsche would have loved this place."

Bobby was a waif in those days, with long hair and delicate fingers and a woolen cap he'd pull low over his head as though it were snowy cold every hour of every day. He wore T-shirts and baggy jeans and scratched at his chin with one of his fingernails—exactly the kind of guy you wouldn't want waiting your table in a restaurant. I'd never encountered this breed of sensitive male, the kind that made love slowly, ate mindfully, and talked about literature.

"That is so Nietzsche," he would say about so many things, and I assumed it was.

When Bobby landed the Adjunct Professor of Epic Literature post at Rice University, he took off the beanie and cut his hair to a God-fearing length. We moved to Houston. My parents were regrouping themselves in Tranquility Oaks. Straightaway, Bobby's emotional circuits began to atrophy. He lost weight. He smoked marijuana, buying it off students. He got eczema on his legs and battled erectile dysfunction. It was like a time bomb had been hidden inside him, ticking away as Bobby approached middle age, and suddenly it detonated.

Rice didn't appreciate him enough, he said. They had him blathering to freshmen. No one in the department had any brains. He ground his teeth in his sleep and his sweet beachy smile turned the color of sand. He began to stay out late, currying the favor of those who drank. There was Victor, the Romantic Poets guy, who drank Bobby into a stupor in our living room, and then followed me into the kitchen with an erection that needed to be shown Bisskit's cast-iron skillet.

Then the English Department asked Bobby to take on a freshman course called The Modern Novel, and he became completely unglued. He threw his chair through his office window, narrowly missing a student on the path below. Later, gnashing his way through a spring semester overview of the Bloomsbury group, it was our glass he broke—six wineglasses—one by one against the kitchen wall.

"You don't get it, Julia. They're keeping me down. The low man on the epic totem pole. They don't want me to outshine them."

Bobby kept his rage burning like Odysseus's soul-flame, buried under the leaves.

"I can't help it," Bobby ultimately told the family court judge.

The judge said, "Help it." Then she slammed her gavel on her block. In that instant, I so wanted to be her, not me—the scolding arbiter, whose life this wasn't. After she said it, Bobby turned to me candy-caned with fury, and I about liquified in fear.

At the same time, I had this veiled sympathy for Bobby. He and his three brothers grew up in a household where all members wished each other dead. They butted up against each other in a deteriorating brownstone on Boston's Back Bay, with ominous cracks in the plaster ceilings and Charles River rats scuffling in the basement. The walls were lined with their father's collection of graduate degrees, and every standing object was decorated with their mother's hand-knit shawls, hand-sewn quilts, and hand-painted silks.

The family spent summers in a kind of camp in the Adirondacks, where there was no plumbing or electricity. Bobby took me up there once. Each house was two stories and the staircase was a whole tree. Wood canoes had been nailed onto the walls for decoration, and the outhouse was vile. People didn't speak to one another unless the butter needed passing.

Bobby's mother died of obesity-related diabetes. She's crushing chairs up in heaven now. Three months later, Bobby's father married a Korean girl, Jie, whom he insisted on calling Jeanie. She arrived like a child mail-ordered from a catalogue, a bubbly little urchin, always pointing to things and asking, "You like?"

Bobby's father died in a car accident within the year and left everything to Jie in his will. The Back Bay brownstone, once deemed a crumbling teardown, was appraised at six million. "Location, location, location," the realtor smiled. Bobby and his brothers sued for Jie's inheritance and lost. She sold the brownstone and moved back to Korea. The house in the Adirondacks was deeded back to the community camp. I never begrudged Bobby his rage.

For me, the question is not nature vs. nurture. The question is nature vs. self-control.

16

Tonight, Hurricane Che is Category 4. It rolled over Turks and Caicos Islands with unimaginable destruction. There are predictions of a billion dollars of damage. Tomorrow it will make landfall in Cuba, where people are stealing plywood from one another's windows. In Haiti, people don't have plywood. They're stealing each other's chickens.

Tonight Gracie and I have electricity. I've used a lot of it by cranking up the air-conditioning, trying to suck away the odors.

I roll up shredded chicken in corn tortillas, secure them with toothpicks, and lay them in a baking dish. I pour salsa and enchilada sauce over the lot of them and sprinkle Jack cheese on top. Tex-Mex is casual architecture with a wide range for error. It's a round-up-the-usual-suspects kind of cuisine. The cheese is inside, the cheese is outside, the avocados are sliced or mashed, the tortilla is open-faced or rolled around some meat. Salsa and pico de gallo—basically the same ingredients, one chopped fine, one chopped coarse. Gracie loves a dollop of refried beans underneath everything.

"Need help?" Gracie asks me as I shove the casserole dish into the oven.

"I'll need help eating. Twenty minutes."

She brings her drawing pad and colored pencils to the kitchen table and we both draw. Gracie draws outfits for princesses. I try to resurrect in my mind what was on the attic walls. We both reach for the pink pencil at once.

"I'm sorry about the paint," she says. Her eyes are instantly glistening.

I lift her onto my lap. "It's just paint."

"But it's Daddy," she says, and crumbles into tears.

"Daddy's not well." My breath catches. I remember my mother telling us that our daddy was in The Clinic. The weight of repeated history is smothering me.

But Gracie is appeased. She goes back to drawing. "I was right about pink, wasn't I, Mama?"

"Yes," I say. "Pink solves things."

She's quiet for a while. When dinner is ready, her appetite is there. We listen to the radio report on Che. I consider running to the supermarket to top up supplies.

"If you're going to pick the chicken out, can I have the tortilla part?" Gracie asks. She makes circles in the air with her fork. Turkey vultures make loops like that above dead armadillos. I push my plate toward her.

"Maybe for Lent," she says, "I'll give up pork chops."

"Lent?"

"All my friends do it."

"Why pork chops?"

She shrugs. "If I give up something I love, I'll be all grouchy." She slugs down her milk. "Like you."

I take a slug of wine.

"How do people get over things?" Gracie asks.

Alcohol. "Things like what, for instance?"

"What if someone hurts you? Do you have to get over it?"

"Are we talking about the paint?"

"Maybe. Maybe not."

"Your daddy is still very, very angry with me. The paint is, for him, proof of how angry he is. He has to get over his anger. I have to get over the black paint. It takes time."

Gracie is quiet for a minute. "But how? How exactly? Is there a *way* to get over hurt?"

I am overcome by sorrow. I stare at my plate. What have I ever gotten over? I've ingested every pain and loss since baby teeth. "This is what I think: sometimes there's not a path to healing, there's only time. Sometimes, even when an injury is very deep, enough time passes, finally, so that other events intervene."

"I don't get it," Gracie says, irritable now, having found herself walking an emotional plank without a clear endpoint.

"When Claire was fourteen years old," I say, "she had a terrible thing happen, and my father caused it, so it was terrible in many ways. I thought I'd never get over it. But the strange thing is, time kept marching on, and over the years things have intervened—like you, like travel and work, like marriage and divorce—and I can think about Claire without…without crying."

"What happened to Aunt Claire?"

"Ask me sometime when there's not so much black paint around," I say.

"Claire never left the bad thing behind."

Gracie has never met her aunt Claire, but she has heard just enough to be dangerous.

"Claire had much more than paint to deal with," I say.

"Like old Mr. Lanier losing his son in Iraq, and then his wife. He won't get over that. He'll die before he gets over that."

"I think you're right."

"So," Gracie concludes. "So some things you just don't get over. You're hurt forever."

Maimed, I think. Throbbing.

That evening, I spray isopropyl alcohol over the attic walls. I rip old bath towels into swatches and massage gobs of heavy black paint off my drawings. Bobby botched his own job. It's a mess, no question, but there are lines to salvage. I fill two lawn bags with rags, caked and murdered. Gracie comes up to help me, but the fumes are too much.

With a fan blasting, I use oil crayons to redraw and rescue lines, pulling my women from the wreckage of an earthquake, arm here, leg there.

Gracie comes and goes.

"Homework?" I ask.

"Did it."

Off she goes.

Later (new outfit), "Do you hate Daddy more now?"

"No."

"Did he ruin everything?"

"You're still perfect."

She disappears. Then reappears in pajamas.

"How do you decide how to feel?"

I look at her. "Sometimes I don't decide. Sometimes my head fights with my heart, and sometimes I just put the issue into a small box with cotton and stow it where I don't have to look at it."

"Don't put off till tomorrow what you can do today," she says, smiling in a rascally way.

"You caught me."

That night, as I lie down with Gracie, she asks, "Is Daddy mad at me too?"

"No," I say. I pray.

WEDNESDAY

17

The next morning, Daddy arrives like a FedEx package. When I open the door, he's propped against the brick.

"Here you go," says the male nurse, the delivery man. He's got one big hand clamped to Daddy's shoulder and one holding a clipboard. The nurse's name tag reads Jamaal. He looks like a linebacker for the Texans. Actually, standing next to my frail and disoriented father, he looks like two linebackers. I want to tell him the body he delivered was once a scouted McAllen quarterback with a scholarship to Columbia, but instead I stare with incredulity.

"You one of the original Calaway clan?" Jamaal asks me. He's checking off boxes on his clipboard. He picks up a small canvas suitcase, which is caved in from emptiness. I remember that suitcase. Daddy used it his whole life for trips to Galveston and New Orleans. He packed that suitcase one last time when he moved into Tranquility Oaks. I pull it into the house. It weighs no more than two yards of Sanforized canvas and a brass zipper might.

Daddy's forehead rests against the brick and his mouth is slightly open. He might be translucent. I haven't seen him vertical for years. It isn't comforting.

"We're descended from those Calaways," I say. "On my father's side. Daddy?" I embrace him. He feels as crushable as a sun hat. "Could you help me get him inside?" I ask.

I envision Jamaal and myself each taking an arm. Instead, with a practiced dip, Jamaal sweeps up my father and carries him over the threshold like a bride. End of simile.

"Where to?" Jamaal pivots left and right, letting Daddy's legs swing loose. My index finger makes a tentative motion toward the living room and Jamaal sets Daddy down on the sofa. Daddy lists ominously to one side. He becomes, in that instant, an issue, not a person, more like a book that needs straightening on a shelf. Sweat breaks out across my body. It's the animal cry I can't let loose.

Jamaal shores him up with pillows, then ties Daddy upright with a cashmere throw that was folded on the sofa. The throw was a Pitti Palazzo experiment into home goods that never got off the ground. They could have marketed it for binding the elderly.

"I'll get the rest of it," Jamaal says, and disappears.

"Daddy?" I say, sitting lightly beside him. I put a hand on his shoulder. His shoulder bone. He's become a science class skeleton. "I'm glad to see you."

There's no reply, not a flicker of acknowledgment, and I have known for weeks, maybe months, that Daddy has passed already, and it is only his heart, well-wired by the surgeons at Methodist Hospital, that continues to pump.

Jamaal reappears and drops a large cardboard box of male adult size-M diapers on the floor. Next to it he sets down a case of chocolate Ensure. There it is, the sum total of my father's daily needs. My mouth opens to say thank you, but I only take in air.

"The Calaway Boys," Jamaal says, "was the ones that dredged out the bayous for boats."

I try and fail to smile. "Oh? I thought the Calaways tried to bilk the Allen brothers out of the Heights."

"I can't really speak to the banking part. But the Calaway boys were the ones who widened the channels all right. Diggers. Maybe they got up to swindling later. I go to night school."

"That's tremendous," I say. I glance at Daddy. Is it okay to tie a man to a couch? Daddy's milky eyes begin a glacial circuit of the room. He's blind, so it might be an inconclusive tour.

"The Calaway bros," adds Jamaal, "was uppity folk."

Oh no. Not even straight history but social indictments, too. "I'm so sorry," I say. Then I stand and head toward the door. Chit-chat over. I'm confirming his allegation.

"We study a lot of Texas history," says Jamaal, unmoved. "Because most of the students come from other countries. The way I see it, you can't just start with Texas. You wanna talk history? You gotta go way back. Say, to the African pharaohs."

"You're right," I say. Panic is fading in like violins. Should I tip him? "Thank you again for bringing my father home."

"King Tut was a black man. Not many people get that."

I glance back into the living room. Daddy, with maybe ten days left on his calendar, is making weird noises.

"They got Tut coming to Dallas. I know we got Lucy here, but nobody connects with a few bones, you know? 'Specially when she looks like a ape. Now Tut's gonna be a real show. Tons of gold." Jamaal stops outside the door, looking at me like he's ready for a new discussion topic for us.

"Did Daddy eat breakfast?" I ask.

"I didn't ax him."

"Guess I'll go do that," I whisper.

"Oh, sure," says Jamaal. "I gotta go too. We had six passers last night. When they told me, I said, 'Six? Seriously?'"

We stare at each other a moment, each of us in a distinct cocoon of shock. Then he nods amiably and turns to go.

Healthy hearts have about one and a half billion beats in them. While he's been over at Tranquility Oaks, Daddy's heart muscle hit its goal and tried to quit, only to have Methodist Hospital restart it, and then brace it with electrical shock and nitroglycerin pills. A few months ago, a bout of flu led to a bout of pneumonia, which led to another long stint in the hospital, which led to a systemic shutdown. His doctors gave him five days. They moved him into hospice care.

At hospice, Daddy had a private room. I taped Remington posters on the mustard-colored walls—Daddy always liked cowboy-and-Indian pictures. Lisa and I sat at his bedside arguing about childhood (*I* was the one with Halloween duty—any memories she had of carrying Claire around the neighborhood came from listening to my vivid stories) and hoping he heard the vague murmur of our affections. Daddy was a shrunken housing of skin and bone. His heart insisted on pumping, although it was the only muscle with any last intention. His brain and sphincter had abdicated. I touched his cheek periodically to see if it was still warm.

Lisa had unearthed a renowned geriatric specialist in Houston, and he arrived in an unassuming package. Dr. Ingram was a short, bald man with a tentative nature and wire spectacles. He visited twice a day.

"Your father may well recover," he'd said, pushing his wire glasses up his nose with a nervous quaver.

To which Lisa had laughed. "And world peace to you, too!"

"Pardon me?"

I grabbed Lisa's elbow and guided her out the door. "This is not New York," I scolded, and we giggled like thieves all the way out to the parking lot.

I liked the tiny doctor, even though he looked as if he might break down at each visit. He was just north of plump and kept his short arms tucked up around his chest like a hedgehog. I could imagine a gift shop selling salt shakers that looked like him.

Lisa and I would watch Ingram in the cafeteria and in the broad linoleum corridors, shaking his shiny, bald head and shedding tears with grieving families. He often turned up in Daddy's room wearing a white lab coat with someone else's name embroidered on the lapel. He led the way for everyone incapable of handling an emotional burden.

"He's adorable," I said to Lisa.

"He must cry all day and write all night, because he's published all over the world," Lisa replied. "I had my secretary track him down. His name is like the Golden Rule of hospice care."

Lisa stayed on for a week, helping me chart out funeral and burial procedures. Each day we went to the hospice building, robotically threading our way from the parking garage to the elevator to the west wing to the Clayton Ward. The smell in the building was so sad, something between disinfectant and disintegration.

"I feel like I'm sitting Shiva already, right here next to Mr. Obituary," Lisa said. "Maybe we ought to hold a preemptive memorial service. I have to get back to New York."

The day after Lisa flew north, a nurse called me to say that Daddy had turned a corner and was wide-eyed and inquisitive. "He's got an appetite and he's smiling," the nurse added. "Hello? Miss Calaway? Are you there?"

I'm here. And now, so is Daddy.

I padlock all review of our family. Of Claire.

The guest room is also off the table. There is no way I can get Daddy upstairs. I'd have to drag him by the feet. The living room couch is not a permanent option, unless I keep him tied down (I study Jamaal's knot). So I find myself, ten minutes later, dragging down the twin mattress from Lisa's old room. *Bump, bump, bump,* and into the dining room. I shove the old maple table and chairs to one side and make up the mattress with fresh linens.

Another dying relative in the dining room. Maybe someday I'll be lying in there, too, counting my last breaths and staring through the french doors at pecan branches full of squirrels. Maybe someone will bring me soft sheets and down blankets and a clock radio, shove the table against the wall, and redetermine this room. The curtains will be lint by then.

In the living room Daddy lists a few degrees starboard.

"Welcome home," I say. I try to catch his gaze, but Daddy's open eyes are doors without visitors. "The Texans play the Colts this weekend, Daddy. They've moved the game to Indianapolis because of Hurricane Che. We've got a new quarterback."

The air-conditioning pauses with a heavy, graceless sigh.

"There's a storm coming, but don't worry," I explain. "You never did evacuate, did you? Only Mother, always threatening to beat a path to Lubbock. I'll latch the shutters tomorrow."

We called our parents Daddy and Mother. Our mother felt that Mom, or Mama, would have suggested she had fornicated.

Through the living room window, I watch a van pull up in front of the Blantons'. The sky is sulfur yellow.

"Mrs. Blanton is throwing one of her soirées tonight," I say. "She built a catwalk over her pool. All the caterers in Houston are stuffing pimentos into olives right now."

Nothingness fills me. I feel like I'm hoeing a thousand acres of depleted soil in the hopes of being pleasantly surprised. I look at Daddy. What of me could possibly have come from this man, all trussed up like one of those strange things you find among your sushi. I undo the cashmere throw and Daddy falls gently against me.

"Let's get you to the dining room," I say. We manage an awkward shuffle. My feet move and his feet drag. I undress him to his white cotton T-shirt and an adult diaper from the nursing home. My mother said you could tell a man's class by the design of his undershirt. No sleeves, no class. Daddy's is a V-neck with sleeves. He has a fresh Band-Aid on his arm, and I wonder if they gave him a sedative for the trip.

"I'll sew you some new shirts," I murmur. Daddy was my very first manikin. He wore all the clothes I sewed for him, no matter the fabric—clowns, cowboy boots, baby elephants with party hats—whatever bolts Universal Fabric had on sale. The hems were uneven and my mother cuffed his sleeves to hide the inexact buttonholes, but he never said a word.

"Thank you for that, Daddy. For wearing what I made you." I arrange his legs under the covers and straighten out his hips. Even beefy football players finally dwindle to a rangy set of bones and joists.

"You were never vain." I glance into the canvas suitcase. Two undershirts, two pairs of boxers that probably haven't been worn in years, a button-down shirt, a pair of pants, three pairs of pilled socks, a ditty bag, stale air.

"You didn't sign any hogwash paperwork, did you, Daddy? I know you didn't. Tranquility Oaks threw you out for the room. I'm sorry for the upheaval." I pull another quilt over him. He has none of the normal blubber that keeps a person warm at room temperature.

"I'm going to get you some lunch, and then I have to work. You're probably tired."

I touch him on the cheek. He is a creature devoid of acknowledgment, an organism given a forward shove eighty-five years ago, gradually rolling to this halt. His skin is soft and crepey. I glance down at my own arms, halfway there. There's still a scar across my left hand where a piece of shattered crystal from one of Bobby's rages made landing.

Daddy puts down a little broth before dozing the day away.

18

Gracie, after school, looks into the dining room and takes note of the modest atoll under the blanket.

"It's not really like having someone else around," she shrugs. "Why are you dressed up?"

"I'm going to interview help this afternoon," I say.

"To help me, to help you, or to help Grandpa?"

For a child, she is handy with the eyebrows. "All three," I say.

"Do I get a voice in this?"

"Yes. If you hate them, I won't hire them." More reckless words were never spoken.

Gracie walks into the kitchen with a swagger in her little gait.

"What am I in the mood for?" she asks herself in front of an open refrigerator. "You never make me smoothies anymore."

"What's the rule about refrigerator doors?" I say.

"But after the power goes out. This is not my first hurricane, Mama."

I slip frozen strawberries, mango, orange juice, and yogurt into the blender.

"Are we moving?" Gracie frowns from the kitchen table. "The counters are empty."

"I tidied up," I say.

"You don't look like you need help." She taps a finger on the counter and examines me. "Maybe if you took off the big barrette."

Was that it? Was my barrette the line between public despair and composure? "I don't want to scare anyone away."

Gracie makes a face that suggests she is the ward of a

moron. "Shouldn't it be the opposite? Shouldn't the kitchen be a mess and your hair all crazy so that the people who come know what they'll have to do?"

"Yes. It should be the opposite," I say. I set the smoothie in front of her, clean the blender and restow it, concealing any last signs of human habitation. "But it isn't."

The doorbell rings with our first candidate from the Oaks Agency. Gracie and I open the door and peer out with the enormous eyes of tomb robbers. On the stoop stands a squat, middle-aged Latina, if fifty-five is the new thirty-five. She looks up at us with an imperious glare: the white men have taken her land and made slaves of her people, but she will prevail. An inner voice wails, *keep her out on the stoop.* The barrette has made my scalp an electrical circuit of pain.

Her name is Carmen. She's the mother of ten children ("Ten! You count 'em!" she commands me), and she pads across the floor into the living room in bright white Keds that somehow indicate, more than anything she might say, that she will outrun my ability to reject her.

We sit down in the living room. It seems more cheerful without Daddy tied to the couch.

Carmen is from Ecuador. This, it must be admitted, is to her advantage. Ecuador is currently the flavor of the month in Houston. Rumors of a strong work ethic are rife. She has short, no-nonsense black hair and a valiant blue belt that trusses her like a plump chorizo. She whips her head left and right, taking her measure of the house, as though she just spruced up Quito and has been urged to address the Julia Calaway shambles next. Her all-business brow says every corner demands bleach.

Carmen speaks just enough English to bully me into out-lining any duties beyond cleaning.

"Go on. Go on. You tell me," she says.

"Well, there might be ironing," I venture.

"Don' worry!" she scolds me dismissively.

"The groceries," I say.

"Don' worry!"

"I ought to tell you about—"

"Bah. Don' worry!"

"—my father."

The interview comes to a strangling close, like that strap of blue leather that wrings Carmen's waist into a nickel's noose. I beckon her to the door half-panicky that she'll re-fuse to go.

"I got the job?" Carmen demands while the door gapes open.

"You've been wonderful. I'll just check the references you gave me," I say.

"Don' worry! I got the job."

"I'll call the agency tonight," I say, and lock the door behind her. Gracie senses that the moment requires a little hip-hop.

"If I hate them, you can't hire them," Gracie beams, big blue eyes dazzled by the excellent rules.

"Of course not," I reply.

"I'm the deciding vote." Cartwheel. Lime-green under-pants with gold stars.

"You are."

"She was too bossy."

"They can't all be like that," I say feebly.

"Don' worry!" Gracie chirps, having excavated the sole morsel of delight from that brief summit of horror.

At four-thirty a light knock augurs the second applicant. It is Immaculada, a thirty-year-old dwarf from Guatemala (note to self: call Oaks Agency with vitriol). Immaculada is the height of our doorknob. She is shorter than Gracie. If you spelled her name in forty-eight-point font, it would circle her hips. Gracie's eyes glom onto this magical image of Miniaturized Adult as though it might be a pet, or a toy, something made of twigs where normally branches are used.

Immaculada is no stranger to people's skepticism. Unable to speak a word of English—apparently a silly suggestion on the agency's application—she leads us into our own kitchen to show how she can climb onto counters to clean cupboards and put away plates.

"See?" She smiles. ¿*Si?* "*Mira.*" *Look*. She takes off her outside shoes and slips on tiny ballet slippers. Then she leaps onto an overturned laundry basket to open the washing machine.

¿*Si?*

I watch. I want to apologize to the world, because I cannot get within a mile of hiring her, even with Daddy residing on the floor, so well within her reach.

At five, we open the door to Maria, a morose Hispanic woman, whose husband is the pastor of an indeterminate church. But times are such, so here she is... She speaks a combination of English and Spanish, punctuated by deep prolonged sighs that bridge the languages of all historic genocides. She has never cleaned homes before, she admits, but there goes that mysterious God for you again. She plods from the sofa back to the front door like the bereaved in a funeral cortege. She is incapable of meeting my eyes, only once glancing up at Gracie and shaking her head woefully, divining that the poor child has only grim, grim days ahead.

At five-thirty, a young Honduran woman comes in and has an allergy attack. I give her Benadryl.

Short prayer: Dear Lord, please don't let her go into anaphylactic shock.

After gulping down a glass of water, she wobbles to the living room on stiletto heels made of Lucite.

"Can you tell me about your prior experience?" I ask. I flash a jaundiced smile and hate myself. What do these women ever see but thin smiles of concealment?

"Ehh," she hesitates. Her name is Esperanza. She is tall. Her face is thin and almond-shaped like a Modigliani model, her lips big and working over an answer. She radiates fear, implying that I might lean over the coffee table and smack her.

"I spick Anglish," she says.

"Right," I say. "Great."

"I do" Esperanza begins. "*Todo*," she blurts out, gesturing her hand in a circle. "I do *todo*."

We talk about the weather. Very caliente. The coming hurricane. *Una tormenta tan grande*. Eventually Esperanza wobbles to the door with nervous gratitude. I break a hot sweat as I consider the medical liability of this sweet creature lurching off her Lucite platforms and splintering her legs on our front steps. Slate. Daddy set them himself thirty years ago, sweeping the extra stone dust into the rose bushes and giving himself a hernia.

"I'll call the agency," I assure Esperanza as she totters toward the street (seven more feet and it will be the city she sues). I make a telephone gesture to my ear, a Texas Longhorns Hook 'em sign to the head. "Thank you so much for coming."

When the door shuts, I sink against it with relief and despair. Gracie, who has skipped into the kitchen for Interview Sustenance, now returns with two glasses of chocolate milk.

"Perfect," I say, settling onto the floor with her. It takes only the sight of this child for peace to bleed through my body. How unfortunate that children don't have the benefit of themselves. They are one-way providers of deep joy. They carbonize love into something ten times harder than diamonds.

"You should design shoes like that," Gracie says gravely.

"Did you like them?"

"Love, love, loved them. And you could bring them to the recycling center afterwards."

It occurs to me in that instant, sitting on Cousin Roy's crap hardwood floor with Gracie, enjoying her chocolate milk mustache, smelling the old wool of an ancient Bahktiar, that our mother never derived pleasure from us. None of us. Lisa, Claire, and I were products she had inadvertently manufactured, then pressed and shipped out the front door.

Mattel took more pleasure in Barbie. Our need for love confounded her. I try to imagine my mother sitting on the floor out of choice.

I unclip my brutal barrette and let go of a brutal laugh that has been carefully cinched into its own proper bow since three this afternoon.

"Madness," I say. I hug Gracie to my side.

"Should I make chocolate milk for Grandpa?" she asks.

"That's nice of you."

"Any more loco-moco housekeepers?" She's perfectly serious.

"One more applicant to go," I say to Gracie.

"Don' worry!" Gracie giggles.

At six o'clock we hear the knock of "the quick girl." That's how Gracie and I come to allude to her. She is eighteen and her Spanish-speaking mother has come along to interpret—not the English, which to the girl is second nature, but the potential devil worship of the unscrupulous capitalist hiring pig (me).

Unfortunately, the girl mumbles, her mother has to stay in the car because her period arrived unexpectedly and she is drenched in blood. I send the girl home with a fresh bath towel and burst into hot fat tears, the kind a child produces. Gracie settles on my lap and pats my back.

"Don' worry, Mama." She has her drawing pad and pen and busies herself drawing a leggy chart. One column is WHO, and there are spaces afterwards for YES/NO.

1. The Bossy One
2. The Tiny One
3. The Sad Woman
4. The Shoes
5. The Quick Girl

"You can just put happy faces or sad faces if you want to," Gracie tells me. "I'll understand." Her hand with its pencil hangs above The Shoes. Gracie puts a happy face in its box. And then, NO.

"I'm not ambivalent," she says. "I'm just being fair about the shoes."

Ambivalent is a big word. It was one of Bobby's favorite words to hurl at me.

"You think ambivalence is some kind of virtue?" he would say. "Flip-flopping? Dunno? Not quite sure? Waffling? You have to feel ambivalent about everything? Is this a gender thing? Women and all their layers again? Well, you know what? Sometimes ambivalence is a bitch, baby."

Bobby was a man designed to be divorced. Toward the end, he maintained that I had stopped him from achieving his life's mission. I asked in the nicest way if he was referring to his fucking Grendel book. We were facing each other in the foyer at the foot of the stairs. He was red-faced and wild-eyed, and I had a sudden appreciation for that blotchy Irish skin that people talked about. Gin-geraniums had blossomed across his father's face until the day he drove into a light post, and his mother had had skin as white as calla lilies—yards of it. When Bobby became angry, cherry fireworks exploded on his cheeks.

I'd begged him to leave the house, for good, again, and some might have interpreted this as support for his professional advancement since he used to call Gracie and me his ankle irons.

"Fine!" he'd yelled. "Fine! But I get the OED. You think you're going to take everything? Well, you can have this old house and you can let it go to ruin all around you. You never lifted a finger to maintain this wreck. You never concerned yourself with anything but yourself. And you know, this is a new world, a world where I'm allowed some satisfaction, too."

I had heard it all before, the same bits and pieces shuffled around under his coconut shells.

He concluded, "I've always come last. You can't fire me, I quit!" Then this one night, after his standard finale, he reached his hand toward his pocket, and I thought, *Thank God, he's going to grab his car keys and go*, but instead his hand whipped out and backslapped my face, slashing it with his ring.

It didn't hurt at first. Mostly I felt the skin relax where the surface tension had been severed. Even before I sensed the warm wet blood sheeting down my cheek, Bobby's eyes rolled back in his head and he dropped, calla-lily-white, to the floor. Gracie came shrieking down the stairs. She ran into my arms and in minutes we were both sticky with my blood. I called 911 and explained evenly that there was a body in my foyer, an abusive husband, who had passed out. Happened all the time, the cops said.

Calmness had cocooned me. The whole thing was re-solved—marriage over, negotiations over. The police drove Gracie and me to the emergency room and they bought Gracie an ice cream cone while I was stitched up by a plastic surgeon.

Fortunately my blood was on Bobby's college ring. It was his alma mater's diamond that ripped my skin. That was more than circumstantial and while I didn't press charges, I requested a restraining order.

If he had hurt Gracie, I would have eviscerated his un-conscious body.

19

The housekeeping interviews are over and there isn't a crippled soul I would consider adding to this dizzy household. The Oaks Agency offers to send over more applicants after the storm but I decline.

Gracie and I settle in the kitchen, Gracie with her colored pencils, me with a glass of wine. I flick on the news. KTRH predicts Hurricane Che will make landfall on Friday evening south of Galveston, anywhere from Corpus Christi to Freeport. People on the coast are wishing the Continental Shelf were a little deeper right now. The warm water is intensifying the storm. More Harris County zip codes are listed for mandatory evacuation. The mayor is debating a contra-flow lane on I-45, but the county judge has urged people to hunker down. All airports are scheduled to close on Friday afternoon. I would give anything to read the tea leaves. Will Daddy be alive Saturday? Will this house be damaged beyond repair? Will Bobby leave Houston before the airports close?

I set water to boil in the kitchen and check on Daddy. He's lying on his back. I don't know if he's asleep or awake. I nudge him a bit and his mouth opens.

"I have vanilla pudding, Daddy."

Each time I bring the spoon to his mouth, his jaw canti-levers open like some kind of mollusk. His eyes are as pearly as oysters. He sips some juice from a straw.

"Does this taste nice?" I spoon pudding into his willing mouth.

Daddy's eyes are in perpetual motion but I don't think they're feeding any data to his brain. His pupils are the size of salt crystals. His irises are cobalt blue and look enameled. Sometimes he makes soft noises, though, with enough mod-ulation to suggest words once lived in his head.

"I'm going to give you a freshening bath," I say. I carry in a pot of warm water. "I put a little bath oil in the water. We'll start with your feet and keep the rest of you covered and warm. This is an afghan that Bisskit knit. Do you remember?"

Remember?

I roll him to one side. It's a modest bed, but it serves the purpose. I don't think Daddy is offended. Sometimes his eyes, on their random flight pattern, seem to rest with concern on the edge of the dining room table. Why is it above me? Why are all the window panes up there?

When he was a boy, he slept on a hammock in the backyard of a brick one-story house, on a patch of hardtack fifty feet from the Rio Grande. At night he could hear goat bells on the far side of the river, and the soft splash of Latinos walking across the rocky riverbed in the darkness. Daddy was the first boy from McAllen ever to go to Columbia. He got on a bus one day—there's a picture in the family album of that bus; it was silver and bullet-shaped with thrilling wings painted on its sides—and disappeared to New York City. He had a pair of pants, two shirts, and some paperwork admitting him to Columbia University on a full football scholarship.

Those McAllen boys waxed the boys from Dallas in the finals, my mother liked to tell us while she spatchcocked a bird. She didn't boast much about Daddy (McAllen was way off her Houston-to-Hollywood map), but she appreciated a good drubbing. The final score had been fifty-one to twelve. It was inscribed on the frame of a picture of Daddy; he's on one knee, his Mc Hi Bulldogs helmet in his hand. Lisa and I used to stare at it with wonder—Lisa maintaining that the hair had to be a wig. The light in the photograph was West-Texas-sharp, making Daddy's forehead bone white and his eye sockets black tunnels to the sixth dimension. He looked like a man who could've dragged a heifer across a corral.

At Columbia he became tall and manly, with a deep stare and a rakish mop, all of which fell out. Our mother liked to grump, "You want to know disappointment? Marry a head of hair."

For the past thirty-odd years, Daddy has lived invisibly. Our mother served him his pills each day with his meals. At the end of his cellular life, Daddy is nothing if not compliant as I ease his arms into a fresh T-shirt and tuck him under the sheets. I look down at his withered face and imagine goat bells in the darkness across the Rio Grande. He'll cross a new river soon.

When I look up, Gracie is watching me from the stairs. Lisa, Claire, and I used to wedge our faces between those banister rails too, watching our mother for signs of emotional filibuster. She knew we hunkered up there, like naturalists observing a feral cat, and she kept her face flat as a chess piece.

I smile at Gracie, shrug, and walk into the kitchen to boil water for spaghetti. She follows behind.

"Does he talk?"

"No."

"Did Aunt Claire forgive him ever?"

"No."

"Do you think Aunt Claire will ever marry?"

"No number three."

"Three is a prime number."

I rinse a handful of snow peas and set them in a dish at the table. Gracie plants herself beside them. She has her drawing pad and pencils.

"I'm never going to marry a man that hurts people," she says.

"That is an excellent plan," I say. I pour a half-teaspoon of salt into my palm and dust it into the hot pasta water.

"When you and Daddy got married, though, you didn't know."

"That's right."

Gracie traces a snow pea and then eats it. She uses the

snow pea outline to form the trunk of a palm tree, feathering out fronds into wooly wonderfulness. A few doves litter her ground. A girl in a pink smock with triangles on it looks out. Gracie's pink pencil pauses above the girl's face. Then she draws a brief, straight line for a mouth. Then she turns to a new page.

"My wedding dress is going to be long, long," she says. She draws a bride. "Maybe I'll design wedding dresses when I grow up."

"Yours will be gorgeous. You have more imagination than I do."

My own dress was ivory silk under a coffee tulle sheath. I sewed it myself, putting the zipper on the side because I didn't think anyone would come help me dress in the anteroom. It was the loneliest moment of my life. Already I'd had second thoughts about Bobby. Then my mother walked in.

She might have embraced me. It was more hands than arms. I'm still not sure it happened. She unclasped her WWJD bracelet and pressed it into my hand. Then she lowered the netting of her swish little mother-of-the-bride hat—"I cannot listen to that organ racket one more minute," she said—and marched off to the front pew to be admired and congratulated.

I was a little in shock. That was the most affection my mother had ever shown me. I stared down at the bracelet. The silver was worn, almost cratered where her thumb had rubbed it mercilessly. I rubbed it, too, as I listened to the organ wheeze through another round of Mendelssohn's "Wedding March." I hadn't designed pockets in my wedding dress, so I slipped the bracelet into my bouquet, where it snagged between the thorny stems of twenty small white roses. Next thing I remember, there was Bobby, poet-delicate, standing stiffly in his morning coat at the altar, waiting for Daddy to trail me aimlessly down the aisle ("Mr. Calaway, the bar is not open yet," they'd said, so he sank down in a pew halfway to the altar).

Later, on the church steps, I closed my eyes and tossed my bouquet and Lisa caught it. I heard a muted *What the hell?* as she fished our mother's WWJD bracelet from out of the roses.

I peer over Gracie's shoulder. Her bride is all alone. There is no groom. But there are puppies. Five of them in various states of dog elation on the bottom of the page.

Gracie's pink pencil hovers above the bride, and suddenly, there is a smile. Then Gracie turns to a fresh page.

"I'm going to make a list," she says. "Of how things should be. Number one: we need a puppy."

She looks up at me. This is not a new conversation. The timing, however, might be ripe.

"You think maybe after the storm?" I say. Huge concession. Sigh.

"Yes! Oh yes!" She noted adjustment in my voice. "Or even before." She's inflated with happiness. She leaps up and does a little happy dance.

"I'll bet the breeders have packed up and left town with all their puppies," I say.

"Well, we don't have blankets or bowls anyway. Want to know rule number two?"

"Please."

"We should have Aunt Claire visit."

My heart skips a beat. "I'm not sure Aunt Claire would like to visit while Daddy is here, but I know for sure she would like to visit when there is a puppy here. That's all Aunt Claire ever wanted when she was a little girl. She had dozens of stuffed dogs."

"Am I like Aunt Claire?" Gracie says.

"You have her beauty. You have her artistic gifts."

"And I'll have dozens of puppies one day too."

Gracie comes to my side. "It's like men do terrible things to women; do women do terrible things to men?"

"I think the pendulum swings both ways."

"Don't let me go," she says.

"Never." I hold her tight. Together we watch pinhead bubbles form at the bottom of the pasta pot and wrench free and rise to the surface of the hot water and disappear into their own mist like freed souls.

20

Over dinner, Gracie twirls pasta around her fork until it's dizzy, then pops it into her mouth. We look through a book of animal photos on loan from the school library. I see polar bears, orangutans, parrots. I sit beside her with my plate and a glass of wine, commenting on the size of everyone's paws. Unconsciously, I shift the glass until it sits between pine knots. This table is as lumpy as prairie sod.

"Do all the animals go to heaven?" Gracie asks.

"That's a good question," I say. "What do you think?"

"I think they should have their own heaven, without leashes and collars. But there would be rules, like lions can't eat baby wildebeests up here."

"That seems fair."

"Can you believe we're going to get a puppy, Mama?"

No. I add puppy to my list of Unimaginables, after Daddy, after Hurricane Che. I cannot help but think of Claire. Claire wanted a puppy the way two hydrogen molecules want an oxygen molecule. Am I addressing Claire's desolation through my own daughter? Maybe, but how do you address your own desolation?

Gracie promises to take care of the puppy-to-be, which is a story older than the Bible.

"Can I come with you to the Blanton house after dinner?" she says. "I can practice playing with their dogs."

"Of course." Mimi Blanton has two poodles named Oil and Gas, who adore Gracie.

I take a last sip of wine and collect my tailor's bag. This is a satchel in which I keep emergency sewing supplies. Needles, spools of seasonal thread colors, snaps, safety pins, Velcro, shears, and a few extra buttons. I've toted this satchel to countless Pitti Palazzo runway shows, from Milan to Bryant Park, for last-minute alterations. It's been to Mimi Blanton's house many times.

Gracie and I are ushered through the front doors of the Blanton mansion at six-thirty. We're immediately caught in eddies of catering people racing in all directions with gleaming silver trays. A man is scolding someone about flowers. A young woman complains about her mascara. I see Mimi Blanton on the upstairs landing, beckoning me to come up the left scroll of stairs.

"I was worried you wouldn't come, darling. Windy popped a button and Stormy's bra is showing. Hello, Gracie. You're getting more beautiful every day."

Gracie thanks her demurely and asks about Oil and Gas.

"I'll have them brought up immediately," Mrs. Blanton says. "They absolutely adore you, you know," she adds, for which I love her a bit. I have layers of years with Mimi Blanton. She has tethered my affection the way a massive oak does, by being there, next door, as though presence alone were nine-tenths of love.

Stormy, Windy, and Sunny are in Mimi's master bedroom, an upholstered boudoir of taupe satins and massive mirrors in flowery gilt frames. They are all three in Pitti. It is pure delight to see dresses I designed in 3D.

Windy, the oldest of Mimi's girls, has big anxious eyes. She is what is casually called a wreck. She married an insurance executive, who is imperturbable, and so she is forced to threaten him periodically with divorce. It seems difficult to get his attention without a full blitz of ultimatums.

Stormy, the middle daughter, makes everyone wonder whether she intentionally moved into her name, or whether her name somehow predetermined her character. She blows through a room like a squall. Even now in Mimi's bedroom, Stormy tacks left and right like she's looking for something, like maybe husband No. 4, to throttle. Stormy is the kind of woman the fashion industry loves. She's vain. She covets all her neighbor's things. She won't accept a gift that doesn't arrive in a very, very small box or a very, very big box. And she loves to throw parties that light up the vast Houston sky.

Then there's luckless Sunny, who got into drugs and alcohol at an early age. She was thrown out of boarding school, then college, and then rehab. It's possible her excessively sweet disposition is a result of a chemically deionized brain. Last year she married a man she met at the Betty Ford dry-out. She was six months pregnant by the time she walked down the aisle. I designed a cream silk wedding dress for her with an empire waist and a sweet gusher of pleats and pin tucks to disguise her waistline from prying eyes. Later I created a few baby clothes for her as a wedding gift. The baby clothes caused an unexpected eruption of desire among Houston's haute set. Ever since, I've been beset with phone calls from women begging me to make clothes for their infants, toddlers, and teens. I would have loved to, but all this happened while I was in divorce court or the emergency room.

Sunny's husband disappeared two months after the wedding, and the marriage was annulled, but Sunny seems not to have noticed. I don't know where the child is.

When we enter Mimi's bedroom, the three girls graciously spring up and coo over Gracie. Stormy, Windy, and Sunny all gave birth to boys and mew longingly at Gracie's hair and disposition.

Sunny gives Gracie an affectionate squeeze. "You're growing like a weed," she exclaims. "But prettier!"

Stormy rolls her eyes and whisks herself away.

"She is," I reassure Sunny. I tuck in a bit of her sleeve facing and finish zipping her zipper. At Pitti Palazzo, there are no hooks and eyes at the top of closures. Instead, MK designed a little bar, like a tiny bridle bit, to finish off the clasps. I click Sunny's into place. Then I undo my satchel on an ottoman that's larger than my living room couch.

Windy rushes up to me in a flutter of unease. She's been

enhanced since I saw her last, and the saline burst the corset seam.

"You look fabulous," I say, threading my needle with grove-green silk thread.

Stormy looks over her shoulder. "Windy is boob-challenged," she laughs.

Windy tears up, suggesting that this is not the first slur of the evening.

"I'm just trying to get back what I lost after the babies."

Stormy snorts.

A maid with a practiced deaf-and-dumb mien walks through the door with Oil and Gas, two toy poodles, and Gracie drops onto the carpet to worship them.

"I'm going to reinforce this seam," I say to Windy. "Do you have a brooch I could use to keep your bra strap from moving?" Windy goes off in search of the house safe. Stormy walks over and gestures to her shoulders. Apparently she's determined to wear a bra with a wide footprint under a silk sheath with angel hair straps.

"Don't worry," she says. "I want the bra to show, I just don't want it to move around."

"I see." From the corner of my eye, I also see Gracie's face swivel toward me. Stormy is like a late-night movie that your parents won't let you watch.

"Madonna had it right," Stormy observes. "You can't get what you want in life if you don't put your bra out there."

I stand Stormy in front of the mirror, where she keeps tossing her head, trying out sexually insolent faces. We compare options. Bra to outside, bra to inside. I could even trellis the bra lace along the straps, but I don't offer, because Stormy is a bitch.

She says, "Windy looks ridiculous with those boobs. Her mammograms are going to be ultra-painful. They've got to shove the saline packets out of the way. Ouch."

Sunny, who is flipping through magazines on her mother's bed, looks up. "Queen Noor had a mammogram."

Stormy makes a noise. She chooses a placement for her bra, ruining the look of the dress and successfully transforming herself into a succubus. I tack everything in place. Windy returns with a diamond brooch so heavy that now I'm thinking it will bring down the silk house. I sew it carefully against her dress, anchoring it to her bra. Gracie watches from the plush carpet, while Oil and Gas lick her to death. I'm done in half an hour and wish the girls a lovely evening.

"You're like an artist with a needle," Sunny murmurs with a smile.

"Fill your bathtubs with fresh water," Windy says.

Stormy swings around to me. "You're not leaving? This storm is massive. It flattened Cuba."

"We're hunkering down," I say. Then I add, although I shouldn't, because comedy isn't my strong point, "Evacuating just encourages hurricanes." No one laughs.

Windy shrugs. "I don't mind the rain, it's the tornadoes that frighten me."

"We love hurricanes," Gracie says, stepping in front of me and lifting her chin up high. "We make forts and eat peanut butter."

"Oh, well then," Stormy replies, her eyes pouncing on Gracie with sheer spaghetti-strapped admiration. "Lucky you."

I can hardly breathe. My child has just stepped forward to protect me from something she could only sense and not see. She did it without thinking, valiantly, realizing that her mother was going to get smushed under the tread of richesse. She slips her hand into mine and squeezes, and I guide us downstairs through the thickening crowd of bodies and out the massive front doors into the thick night air.

We can still evacuate. We can settle Daddy in the back seat of the Volvo and drive to Austin, or San Antonio, or Dallas and sit out the storm in a hotel. It's just never been our way. Should it be our way?

"We need a shaggy rug like theirs," Gracie says as we crisscross the Blanton lawn to avoid roses.

I look up at the lavender sky above the Blantons' blaze of incandescent light. What does Gracie think, wandering through the Blantons' lavish rooms and across their baronial lawn to our modest old house? Does she envy them their mirrors and diamonds and servants and space? Does she feel like the poor tailor's daughter?

Gracie says, "Lucky we can get dressed by ourselves, right, Mama?"

A strangely wonderful heat flushes through me. "Right you are."

"When I grow up, I'm going to be a dog-walker. After the hurricane, I'll ask Mrs. Blanton if she wants to hire me to walk Oil and Gas."

"That's a great idea."

"So I can be ready for our puppy."

I settle Gracie in bed and check on Daddy. He is silent. Immobile. Right now he seems like the least of my worries.

It takes forever to get to sleep. I look out the window to the heavy yellow moon. It's a Sturgeon Moon, the harbinger of autumn. Growing up, there was a boy in my class, Lamar LeBeau, who fished every weekend. His daddy owned a tract of oily sand down Stuart Road in Galveston. All the other kids razzed him for his cracker sunburns, which he got from a mullet haircut, a fishing cap, sunglasses, and a cut-off T-shirt. Lamar was the one who told me about the Sturgeon Moon. He said it signaled the moment when the fish began biting again in Christmas Bay. Not prom conversation, but I never laughed (I sometimes nodded off). He said the August moon was the only moon dedicated to fishermen, unless you counted the March moon, which was the Worm Moon (zzzzz). Lamar was nuts for fish, didn't give a Texas peach for fast cars or football, and twenty-five years later he sold that West Beach acreage for sixty million dollars.

I'm curled up like a possum under my quilts when MaryJane calls the house. I notice it's ten p.m. I need a new bedroom clock—one that doesn't tell me the truth—and a phone that goes silent after eight.

"I'm at the airport," MaryJane announces. "I've had some second thoughts."

"About Paris?" I yawn. Do I sleep too much, or are people conspiring to keep me awake? "You're where?"

"At the airport."

Is Bobby there?

"I need a favor," MaryJane says. Then she whispers, "Shut up a minute" to Emma. "I need you to—do you have a pen? I need you to call Cici and tell her, 'Carraba's breaded asparagus spears for the appetizer.' And I need you to call my housekeeper, Ping, and tell her, 'Twenty.' That's it—twenty. No more. Thanks, Julia. I owe you big-time. They're telling us to turn off our phones and I just panicked, and Mickey isn't answering any one of his numbers. Bon voyage! We'll bring you back a little something from Paris, and good luck with the storm. Can I call you if I need to?"

"Of course."

I trained in Paris after I graduated from Parsons. When MaryJane tortures French, my lungs seize.

I leave the message for Cici, who has evacuated to Austin already. For that matter, she probably saw the writing on the wall about Carraba's asparagus spears before she left. She is co-hosting the school's Christmas festival with MaryJane, which is like trying to share the Oval Office. Thank goodness Cici's got a son, because Emma has been the Virgin Mary in the Christmas pageant since she could walk.

I ring MaryJane's housekeeper next. "Ping, it's Julia Calaway. MaryJane just called from the airport. She asked me to tell you twenty."

"No twenty-five? No twenty-two?" Ping wails in her clipped, just-out-of-the-Hanjin-container accent.

I check my notepad to be sure. My eyes are teary with yawns. "'Twenty,' she said."

"Ya?" She slams down the receiver.

Ugh. MaryJane! I fume.

I fall asleep in my clothes and dream about black, black dresses.

21

Suffering is cubist. It is a slashed mock-up of perspectives and injuries. I dream about Bobby screaming, Claire's frightened eyes, a corduroy skirt I sewed in seventh grade, a drop of black paint, a puddle of blood. I hear my mother weeping in frantic despair, Claire shrieking at everyone to stay back, and the police coming to take Daddy away.

Let me go!

Bisskit had died by the time Daddy walked into Claire's room and pinned her to the mattress. Bisskit would have castrated Daddy in the bathtub and shipped his nuts to Guam.

For the first weeks, Daddy disappeared, first to a lock-up, and then to a psychiatric clinic. My mother bought dead bolts at Southland Hardware and screwed them into all our bedroom doors. Claire got two. Her door remained closed. She employed her new dead bolts with a bone-rattling slam. At night she crept out and burned things in a heap in the backyard. Every morning there were fresh ashes. Once I found scraps of a white bed sheet, later some fabric I'd used to make her a pillow, often the edges of photographs. Our house was just a mirage of shelter.

Then the headmaster at St. John's called to say Lisa was welcome at Miss Porter's School. He sent her home with a foldout brochure.

"You get five feet of snow in the winter and you have to shovel your way forward," Lisa said, eyes wide. She wasn't scared at all. Lisa was always courageous. "Everyone wears huge coats like it's Siberia and mittens and hats. I haven't figured out what to do about my hair yet. Not with those big hats. But if I do my nails at night, they should be dry by morning and I can wear the mittens."

"Will I have to go too?" I said, shuddering with the thought of choosing the devil I didn't know.

Lisa betrayed a look of pity. "Maybe when you're older."

"I want to go to fashion school," I said.

"That's the thing. No fashion classes at Miss Porter's. They're going to help me get into college."

"I'll stay with Claire," I said. There was silence in my head. "I'll just stay."

The next day, I looked out my window onto the backyard. There were the ashes of Claire's recent fire. Something that had been pink was curled into grizzled black and gray. Our mother took Lisa to Foley's to buy cold-weather clothing. I made a desperate attempt to stop the fatal hemorrhaging of everything I thought I knew. I tiptoed down the hallway to find Claire.

She had her dead bolts in place. Inside, her radio was set to loudest.

"Who made a bonfire on our pitcher's mound?" I called through the door, wishing I could make her laugh. "Can I come in, Claire? Claire? Don't leave me out here. Lisa's going away to boarding school. Don't leave me alone."

The music dimmed. "Where's Lisa going?" Claire asked. I could tell she was on the other side of the door.

"I don't know. North. To Connecticut."

"Lucky Lisa."

"Can I come in, Claire?"

"Go away, Julia."

"Can't we be together? I'll sew you a new pillow. I've got lots of fabric."

Silence.

"I can't make it alone, Claire." I slumped to the floor, leaning against her door.

"I'm going to run away, Julia. As soon as I can. You should go with Lisa."

"I'm not smart enough." I knew.

"Then don't. Just stay here in hell."

"Don't you leave me too, Claire," I begged.

And then Lisa was gone, and no one spoke anymore. My mother turned to me once, revved to ream me out because of a stain on a white blouse. Her mouth was open and the air was in her lungs, and in an instant I saw her expression go into arrest. She couldn't yell at me the way she used to yell at Lisa. I couldn't handle it.

Daddy floated through the house like a zeppelin. I used his empty pill jars for my pins and buttons. The day Parsons sent me a letter of admission I nearly fainted with terror. I was a lifer. All I knew was being an inmate.

Let me go!

THURSDAY

22

I've been through plenty of hurricanes. They don't last too long. That's what they say about rape too. Close your eyes. Go limp. Doesn't last long. Maybe someone gave New Orleans all that good advice. It's still limp.

More good advice is blaring over the radio waves this morning. Water, batteries, plywood. Some things are certain: that we will lose power and plants, that the extent of water damage will surprise us, that invisible winds pack the muscle of tidal waves. The ancillary peculiarities, like black iguanas in your driveway, or Jefferson Parish decamping to your neighborhood, are never foreseeable.

Right now, I'm grateful for clear skies because they mean Bobby will have been able to fly to Boston. As I rub the sleep from my eyes, the first thought on my horizon is a happy one: Bobby is far, far away, so I have only a hurricane to worry about. I stretch contentedly under the covers before I remember that Daddy is downstairs.

Daddy!

I race downstairs and into the dining room and put two fingers to Daddy's dry throat. It's warm. He's so quiet it's like having a goldfish around. I'd imagined we would communicate somehow, that he would make a gesture or a noise that triggered memories. But maybe his silence is enough. Maybe it's best.

Before waking Gracie, I give him a warm sponge bath. Then I sit beside him while I drink my coffee.

"I don't suppose you drink hot coffee," I say. "I'm cooling a cup for you in the kitchen. I tell you what, Daddy. I'm going to believe that you were sentenced and served your time in prison and now you're on parole. I'm not your judge or your warder. What you did is the worst thing anyone could do, but I can't help feeling that chemicals were involved somehow, which is not to exonerate you. Only to say you've been nine-tenths altered my whole life, and now you're nine-tenths gone."

This morning, breakfast is cinnamon toast. I break a slice into crumbs for Daddy and help him wash it down with tepid coffee. I don't think too hard about how he chews or what goes down. Nobody should be a health nut on the way out. Above all, I'm grateful for hot food. When a storm hits, electricity is the first thing to go.

Gracie plods sleepily down the stairs (*thump, thump, thump,* like a peg-leg pirate). She's wearing a princess blouse and a jumper on backwards. She flicks on KTRH to listen for school closing announcements, and prays that her own school has locked its doors and submitted its name to be broadcast.

"How annoying," she concludes after a half-hour. We'd heard the ten-minute update three times.

"They're open with a skeleton crew," I say. "It's going to be a morning of games."

"It's still school," she says.

The school is open this morning to give parents more time to prepare for the hurricane. I feel guilty sending Gracie. My mother regularly locked us out of the house so that she could clean in peace. Lisa, Claire, and I played in the bayou, pretending we were penniless orphans left on the village outskirts for feral dogs.

Hurricane Che is about 250 miles offshore and approaching us at fifteen miles an hour. The television shows lines of anxious people grabbing water jugs and crackers from grocery shelves. Traffic helicopters drone in the sky, fomenting freeway panic. In my own little nutshell of anxiety, I walk out to the garage to triple-check our emergency supplies.

Scientists say Texas will get the global warming double-whammy—severe droughts interspersed with absurdly heavy rains. Hurricanes will get stronger, because of warmer waters. We're looking at a future of bottled water and water moccasins under the porch. The Berrys swear a nine-foot alligator moved in under their house after Hurricane Rita. That doesn't seem like a tough thing to substantiate.

Gracie gathers her shoes and socks with a sense of great injustice. The air is edgy and crackly right now, or maybe I am. On the way to school, Gracie testifies that my Grouch quotient has been rising steadily.

"No one would have noticed," she snaps, when I suggest turning her jumper around right-side-forward.

Bisskit used to send my mother and Aunt Loretta to school in belted pillowcases. My mother was mortified, bug-eyed with rage and humiliation; Loretta stood awkwardly beside her, already one club foot into Guam. I've seen the old photos, and the pillowcases weren't all bad. They had scalloped hems. Bisskit had shaped the shoulders with darts. My mother nurtured a resentment against her childhood poverty that could've sunk the USS *Mississippi*.

"Nobody else has to go to school today," Gracie growls through a long and slow-moving carpool. Finally, she leaves me with a curt goodbye, and I watch her skip off to catch up with a friend, big smiles gleaming across both faces.

I drive over to Woodbar and order coffee and a breakfast taco. It feels sacred, walking into a well-lit cafe, as though it's my last foray into the world of hot foods, cold foods, and bright lights before Che arrives and sends us back to tiki torches. In twenty-four hours, not a store will be open. In twenty-five hours, Reliant Energy will abdicate all responsibility for power.

I grab a newspaper and muffle a shriek of delight. Lisa's promotion made the *Wall Street Journal*. There, pixilated in the sixth column is my Lisa's slyly smiling face. Her bangs are blown sideways and she looks out at the reader mischievously from the newsprint.

"Lisa Calaway is being hailed as a long overdue antidote

to Silverman-Shaw's antiquated hierarchy. She is prized as bringing common sense and uncommon shrewdness to complex negotiations, and is not afraid to turn down even the market's sexiest deals if she doubts the reliability of the numbers. Calaway's savvy in the post-recession era has since been proven out."

My inner cheerleader is waving her pompoms. I read the article avidly. I want to show it to everyone in the café. Lisa's boss years ago, Proctor Hadges III, threatened to fire her for repeatedly turning down equity bundles. In 2013 the debt crisis forced banks to liquidate substandard holdings; Lisa's deals were the few black atolls in a sea of red ink, and Hadges was reassigned from head of Equity Investments to Assistant Director of North American HR.

My cell phone rings.

"Do you like the bangs?" It's Lisa.

"I love them! I'm going to get bangs for Gracie."

"It's a little over the top, and they got some of it dead-wrong. Hadges emailed me wanting to know if I hired a PR firm. The bastard."

"I thought Hadges disappeared," I say.

"Hadges is the brother-in-law of someone on the Board," Lisa replies. "He'll never truly disappear. He was only cryogenically frozen in HR. Last week I worried that he might try to interfere with this promotion."

I remember Gracie asking about men being awful to women.

Lisa says, "I spotted Hadges schnogging the girl at the glove counter in Barney's. Very indiscreet for a married creep. Have your rain poncho ready?"

"I'm at Woodbar," I say. "It's not raining in here. And the bangs are totally swish."

"Ooooo, big kudos from my favorite fashionista. Tell Gracie I love her. Wish me luck," Lisa says.

"I will. I do."

"I'll fly down as soon as the storm is over. Oh, and I told Claire about Daddy."

I stiffen unconsciously. "What did she say?"

"It was odd," Lisa reflects. "She said, hmmm, which is one more m than I usually get. Ta-ta."

I returned to the *Journal* article. Hadges was mentioned and even quoted on page fourteen as dismissing Lisa's promotion as political favoritism. He said if he were in a position to fire her, he still would. I could sense his bitterness shrouded in the ink. Like I could feel Bobby's fury buried in that black latex paint.

23

In my attic studio, two fans push air toward an open window. The odor clings to the wood and wall and fabric. I throw a plastic tarp over a cutting table and put my laptop on it.

The black paint missed a few boxes underneath the tables, in which I keep folders full of fabric and gimp and ribbon and notions specs. I have cardboards covered in button samples and embroidery snippets. Fashion design is one part inspiration and seventy thousand parts precise annotation. I look through to see what is salvageable, what might be handy for the new resort collection. After two hours I stretch and take a break by clipping the seams of Gracie's stained school jumper. I lay out the pieces on some Macgillivray tartan that I keep under Gracie's bed. I love the simple seams of children's clothing. Gracie's jumpers are like walking A-frames. If I don't mimic the princess bodice seam across the chest, no one notices. If I don't use a hidden zipper, same. When I trained in the Parisian ateliers, one teeny *désagréable* stitch would cause alarms to go off. *Zut! Zut! Mon dieu!*

A pair of eight-inch Gingher pinking shears survived Bobby's rampage. A box of pins. The cotton is sweetly pliant. I ease the armholes into my sewing machine. In an hour I finish the neck and armhole facings and have the fronts pinned to backs. I'm eyeing some precious pink ribbon that I want to sneak onto the hemline, when the phone interrupts me and Caller ID indicates Gracie's school. I suspect they want to send the children home early.

"Hello?" I say.

"We have Gracie's father here, Miss Calaway. He says he is evacuating the hurricane with Gracie. There are strict rules that you be notified and your permission granted."

A shard of ice plunges into my chest. My hands go clammy and I'm vaguely aware of several nickel-plated basting pins piercing my palm and fingers.

"No," I say, seething with the rage of Caliban. "It's not all right. I'm coming to pick her up."

As I hang up, I hear his furious roar.

It's 2019. I'm sure the school receptionist films the ugly confrontation on her smart phone.

"You may not take Gracie," I hiss. "You may not touch me. You may not…" I have an out-of-body earful of myself listing the laws of our relationship, rebuilding bramble by briar the supposedly impregnable hedgerow of our separation. This man, with whom I once fell in love, with whom I lived for a dozen years, stands before me as a hostile stranger. Do scientists know what happens when love disappears? Do pheromones undergo a magnetic repolarization? Who is this man tilting backward from my gales of anger? And who am I, author of this incredible rancor?

"You're putting Gracie in danger," Bobby says. "Only a fool would ride out this hurricane."

"We. Will. Be. Fine."

"You couldn't protect an elephant from a mouse."

"Why don't you put that in a book and self-publish it?"

Bobby has grown a tufted goatee. He smells of cologne, reminding me of women who, when jilted, change everything possible about themselves. Bobby has put on weight too. He leans toward me and swivels his face away from Gracie. "You're a controlling, manipulative bitch," he spits, his eyes darkening into hurricane blue.

"Did I splash black paint across your office walls?"

"You deserved it."

"I divorced you. What I deserve is to be done with you. And I will call the police if you ever come into the house again."

"You'll need the police."

I swing my head around, wishing someone else has heard him. But there is only Gracie, tiny and pale, hunched up on a school chair. I purse my lips. "You lied to me about Boston," I say. "You lied about Harvard."

That reaches him. His skin mottles in a celebration of fury and humiliation. But he proclaims for Gracie's benefit, "I'm flying out tonight."

"I don't believe you," I say. Immediately I see the familiar body language, the tightening of his upper back, the hitch of one shoulder, the tension down his right arm and the fist waiting at its end. But his eyes flick toward the school receptionist. This is a world of cameras.

"You're a failure as a mother. Everyone knows Gracie takes care of you."

We're interrupted by the appearance of a security guard.

"It isn't going to end here," Bobby says. He swings around to Gracie and kneels before her. "You know Daddy loves you." He kisses her on the forehead and then bounds down the stairs.

The school bell rings. My heart pounds. I offer Gracie my hand, but she recoils. I don't remember getting the two of us into the car. By the time I pull into our driveway, I'm legally blind with agitation. Gracie is around the bend, feeling the wave-force of life's complexity. She unleashes herself into the house, where she promptly flies to her room and slams the door. A tidal surge has this effect, a thick path of sodden devastation, a wake of desolation.

I wander into the dining room and lower myself onto Daddy's soft mattress. Beyond the french windows doves douse for wet bugs in the grass. A squirrel excavates a pecan. I wish Daddy's serenity were contagious. He sleeps all day and night, on his back, his mouth ajar, really the perfect house guest.

I can feel anger working on me.

"I'll be right back," I say to Daddy, which feels a lot like mumbling to myself. "I'll be right back," I shout upstairs to Gracie, who replies with silence.

That old phrase, "The air will do you good"—it wasn't a Houstonian who coined it. Maybe Grendel's mom said it when he slunk from the banquet butchery.

Outside, a billow of humidity wraps around me. I make a mental note to cut the only two hibiscus blossoms before they're whipped off to Waco.

I look around the neighborhood. Judge Garwood, the bankruptcy magistrate, shuttered up and drove to his place in Brenham a few days ago. He's a Presbyterian. Bisskit used to say the Presbyterians were the worst—always smothering their steaks under white gravy. My mother used to grumble about Judge Garwood's never offering us grapefruit from his tree. Am I just the next in a line of spiteful Calaway mothers? Grendel's mom was the real monster, but only out of motherly love.

There were a few suffery things my mother was intent on sparing us. When we were sick, she wrapped our aspirins in raisins, or stuffed them into grapes, or dissolved them into Coke syrup. For special occasions she brought us to Jamail's bakery where warm donuts exhaled between our fingers, and kolaches bubbled with poppy seed filling as black as crude. On weekends, she would make us bird-in-the-nests with the week's stale bread. She fried the bread, then poked out the center, broke the egg into the hole, and sprinkled it with crunchy white granules of kosher salt. She cooked those nests until the egg yolks were hard as lemon drops because she was so sure fatal bacteria lurked in all three corners of the food pyramid. Then she mashed the whole beautiful buttery thing down with her steel spatula as if it needed ironing, too.

Sometimes, when we were little and controllable, she took us to Luby's Cafeteria. Claire loved the pecan pie, and Lisa loved the meatloaf, and I loved the soup. Unfortunately, our mother could not manage a meal there without stalling at the cash register to gasp with affront as each of our dishes got rung up.

"Wait! Wait one minute," she cried out. "This? You want a nickel for this skinny piece of corn syrup and nuts? Do you want to drive honest people away? And this pork chop," she went on. "You cannot be serious. Fifty cents? Did you fry it in a platinum pan?"

The phlegmatic cashier, an enormously fat black woman wearing a hairnet, waited her out. Finally, our mother was forced to open her wallet to this revival tent of sinners. Lisa, Claire, and I, rigid with horror and red with embarrassment, trailed behind her to a table smack-dab in front of the condiments counter so she could stuff napkins and ketchup packets into her handbag.

In between affection episodes, we retreated to our rooms.

24

I walk over to the Berrys' house. Way down the street a station wagon backs out of a driveway with a bundle lashed down on its roof. There's not another soul around. I might be the only person left on earth—well, me, Gracie, because she's my unfortunate ward, and Daddy, who's one-fifth. The street has a post-apocalypse feel. Comfort is a spatter of hammering a few streets over.

Tomorrow is the big day. Twenty-four hours of electricity left. I want to plug in a million appliances for the comfort of watching their lights blink. Behind locked doors and duct-taped plate glass, people determined to see it through take knickknacks off shelves and roll up bath towels at the foot of their doors. Anxious men re-caulk their sills and move furniture away from windows. Bands of plucky tradesmen nail plywood sheets onto windows for a hundred dollars a pop. Hopefully my Jesús is out and about doing odd jobs and filling his pockets.

The fat Phoenix palms that line our street like plump Corinthian columns have survived the worst hurricanes. The sagos, low and clenched to the sod, cope. Texas oaks are thick and gnarled, but their root systems are as flat as salad plates. In storms their branches churn relentlessly like sea hydra, and it's impossible to predict if they'll tip. I scan the neighborhood for loose objects. Mailboxes, swing sets, dogs, tires, bathtubs, have all seen flight time on our street.

Hurricanes are like baroque operas—you know sooner or later you'll be in hell. Tomorrow the lights will go down on Houston. But right now...right now, the sound of a freight train gains on me.

I look up. An enormous gun-gray helicopter is landing on

Mimi Blanton's back lawn. Everybody evacuates in their own modest way.

The Berrys used to stay for hurricanes. They were afraid of looters. Jack slept downstairs on the foyer floor with his pistol under his pillow. The Berrys are getting up there, year-wise. Jack is convinced he's going to be kidnapped and he wants to move to a subdivision with a guardhouse and a gate.

"Everyone from Fort Worth thinks they're going to be kidnapped," Mrs. Berry sighs.

I wonder if Mrs. Berry feels lonely, trapped in her existence with an addled old man and three boys, all grown, with children and prison records. The Berrys were not bad parents, and the boys' revolving-door syndrome at the Huntsville Unit lockup is a testament to what you can't control in life, and maybe that's what makes Jack think kidnappers have set their rifle-sights on him. Because, you can't figure.

I knock on the Berrys' door, just to be certain. They have a scented orange tree in a pot on the veranda. It's too big for me to lift, but it isn't too big for Che, so I tip it and roll it into a corner. Hopefully the hurricane will not deliver it into one of my upstairs bedrooms with an explosion of wood and glass. I need to stand a moment and inhale its perfume. Images of having to speak with Gracie about the school confrontation disintegrate while my sinuses are being dazzled. Is that aromatherapy? My mother said aromatherapy was someone else cooking the dinner.

Our house looks pretty from here. Brick and wood trim, a sweet period at the end of the cul-de-sac. Daddy's bougainvilleas look attractive by the front door. He put them in after he recovered from setting the new front stoop. A hernia is just a fancy word for a rip, Bisskit told us before she died. Her anatomy lessons included that a penis is just a pipe.

The hernia doctor told Daddy no more heavy lifting, so he took to planting flowers everywhere, buying flats of scrawny sale flowers and spending hours punching holes in the St. Augustine for each soil plug. He gardened when he quit dove-hunting, and he gardened in the same way he used to hunt—sunrise to sunset, outside and alone and not blabbing up his recital of Tudors and Stuarts to anyone. Remembering makes me think there was a kind of latent passion inside Daddy, a fervor that got itself tamped down and straight-jacketed and finally euthanized for the good of others.

My cherry tomato pots take a space inside our garage. I latch the plantation shutters, shut off the outdoor spigots, and snip the two hibiscus blooms.

"It's here or Waco," I tell them. They start to wilt before I'm back inside the house.

Daddy is still breathing when I come inside. Every hour is a strange little biological success story.

Daddy dubbed the years behind him his lower fifty, his lower fifty-one, his lower fifty-two, ticking off the birthdays as though they amounted to an interest-bearing ranch loan. He used to say that the real estate behind him was multiply-ing in value all the time. That's a nice way to look at your past, not as a landfill but as a developer's dream.

My mother did well for herself in the death department. She saw the melanoma—I know she did—and let it ride. A little morphine later and she took the ferry over. I'll bet she never once looked back. You can get bone-tired of life.

I pull furniture away from windows and put rolled-up towels by the doors. Each time I walk through the house I see Daddy, lying on his mattress, eyes open, eyes closed, mouth open, brain closed. If I bend to check for a pulse one more time he'll probably summon a scream. I break up bits of sugar cookie for him. Apple juice goes down. I mention the hurricane, but Daddy, as Bisskit liked to say, is twenty miles west of Discussions, TX.

If I had a spine, I'd be furious with Ramzi, but I don't, so I'm not. I'm just completely bewildered. Tranquility Oaks is one of those Last Restaurant on the Turnpike nursing homes, the full-care three-building, here-to-eternity plan.

It's not a low-rent Whataburger operation. It took all my parents' life savings to meet the bills. They applied to the Independent Living unit, and shortly thereafter my mother determined that getting out of bed wasn't her style anymore. They moved to the Assisted Living building, to separate rooms. Neither was a squeaky wheel. My mother made them some good money, dying quick. She never made it to Building 3 with the other steady-state, bedridden residents. She outran them. I thought Daddy was hot on her heels, but his heart seems determined to go it alone.

When the hurricane has passed, Daddy may have passed too. I fish through some papers and call Dr. Ingram, our wonderful weepy hospice doctor. They page him and I make Gracie cucumber sandwiches (no crusts)(peace pipe) while I wait.

"Miss Calaway?" Ingram's gentle voice comes on the line.

"Thank you for taking my call. It's about my father."

"How is he? He's one of the rare patients that leave here in an ambulance, not a hearse. And how are you, and your sister? Lisa, wasn't it?"

"Yes. I—"

It arrives like my own personal Che. A wall of tears trounces me. *Whomp!* I didn't see it coming. Like the Great Storm of 1900. No warning. A monster of a compound sob.

"It's all right, Miss Calaway," says Ingram comfortingly.

I'm drowning in tears. "I'll call back when I can speak."

"I have time," he says. "It's completely understandable."

"They threw him out of the nursing home, Dr. Ingram."

"What?"

"They threw him out. My father. They said he signed a form, that he refused to evacuate, and that he can't come back."

"Then where is he?"

"He's here. He's home with me." A second round of tears surge the field like linebackers. "And the hurricane is coming.

And I have to keep my ex-husband away from my daughter. I thought he was going to Boston. But anyway the nursing home just left Daddy on my doorstep and I don't know what to do. I'm scared," I add, in a whisper. I dissolve like a lozenge in hot water. I thought I'd forgotten how to cry. I thought Bobby's slaps had sealed my tear ducts.

"And why did he leave the nursing home?"

"They said he signed a Refusal to Evacuate form, and because they released him to me, he can't come back without reapplying. It's just impossible."

He says, "It's rather late. I'll stop by tomorrow to check on your father. Let's talk then about the nursing home. We can talk about everything."

His voice is supremely soothing. I thank him, then drench a kitchen towel in cool water and blot it on my face. Why do you have to pay people to be nice to you?

I arrange Gracie's cucumber sandwiches on a tray with a glass of chocolate milk. Out the back window, our measly patch of lawn is a junkyard of toppled bikes and whiffle balls. They are the last things to be secured in the garage. Dirt patches and scraggly overgrown asparagus ferns define our playing field, and for one split-second, I think I see Bobby behind Mrs. Blanton's rose hedge.

Paranoia was my mother's BFF, and I have tried to fend it off my entire life. She thought the men who packed our groceries at Kroger's were professional apple-bruisers. She thought trucks had magnets under their hoods that drew cars into them. She thought that President Kennedy's assassination was a plot by the Chinese to invade southeast Texas; that brown recluse spiders were put in our shoes by displaced Indians; that the milkman was poisoning our milk; and that everything caused cancer—bubblegum, fluoridated tap water, loud voices, old chard, jazz music, bee stings, laundry detergent....There are so many ways to exhaust yourself, and my mother picked a doozy.

I shake my head. I can see through the lacy roses. Bobby's not there. No one is out there. I've got storm nerves.

Upstairs, a buck naked Gracie is listening to the weather report on KTRH. They expect Hurricane Che to stall over Galveston tomorrow at noon, making a mortar and pestle of the island. KTRH was one of Houston's first radio stations. The call letters stood for The Rice Hotel and the station used to broadcast from the hotel roof. Lisa and I would bike downtown and loiter around The Rice Hotel hoping to be interviewed as "someone on the street." We had opinions (Lisa did) and we waited patiently for KTRH to ask us for them. Which they didn't.

Gracie has exhausted herself with tears. I gather her sweet form into my arms. We apologize. I am continually amazed how, with Gracie, you can get to the other side of a clash so quickly. It's to her credit.

"Why do grown-ups get to make all the rules?" she asks. Again and again and again.

"I used to wonder the same thing," I say. "My mother used to put lists of rules on our refrigerator door. She made them sound like the Ten Commandments."

"What did she put on her list?"

I think back. "Keep your chin one foot above your dinner plate."

"How did she measure?"

"With a steak knife."

"What was another rule?"

"Don't pass a blind man on the street or he'll shoot you."

"Is that true?"

"I hope not."

"Grown-ups are annoying."

"Why don't you and I make a list of rules together? We can tape it to the refrigerator door."

This idea is greeted with zeal. Gracie gets a fresh white piece of paper from her drawing pad and writes RULES at the top just like my mother did. Gracie writes: #1. Then she pauses to think, and while she thinks she puts down eight cucumber sandwiches. I stroke her hair. What is happiness? This sliver of a minute.

There was one day. I don't remember what prompted it. Claire painting the kitchen with cocoa mixed in corn oil? Lisa hemming a dress too short? My practicing the clarinet? Were we recalcitrant about chores, or was it just one of those days with three irritating teenaged girls all home sick, vomiting, coughing, crying, feverish, whining? All of a sudden we saw our mother plod decisively downstairs like Nixon about to resign. She had a piece of paper in her hand. Lisa and I hid behind the banister and Lisa whispered that our mother was leaving, finally, and this was her will and she was bequeathing everything to Catholic Charities except a hundred dollars to fix Lisa's nose, which, Lisa noted, wouldn't pay for one nostril.

Our mother walked into the kitchen, stirred a bit, then walked out the back door and started clipping the oleander, a little here, a little there, shearing, pruning, until there were only oleander stumps. Oleander memento mori. Lisa and I tiptoed into the kitchen and immediately we saw it. The imperative bright white piece of paper taped to the refrigerator door. Our mother had heard about Martin Luther nailing his reforms to the church door and she saw herself in the same momentous historical context, a reformer against all odds. Her nail was Scotch tape and the refrigerator was her Wittenberg Cathedral.

RULES, it said on top.

#1 Thou shalt not chew ice or write piss-poor thank-you notes

#2 Thou shalt not take food upstairs or smoke—and I will know

#3 Thou shalt not hem your skirts like sluts

#4 Thou shalt not speer food with your fork

#5 Thou shalt not desecrate this house

#6 Thou shalt converse pleasant-like over dinner
#7 Thou shalt not chew gum or drink brown fizzy stuff
#8 Thou shalt not pour catsup on a good dinner
#9 Sunday is for church or you are doomed to hell

We got off light. Only nine rules. It was Claire, of course, who later mentioned that Martin Luther had challenged the papacy, our mother's Holy Grail. And our mother replied, "Don't worry, Claire. There's a hell for him too."

Nice, pleasant-like conversation.

Threatening us with hell was something our mother did regularly, which goes to show that even hell—flaying fires and malevolent imps into perpetuity—can become hum-drum from overexposure. She said there were certain rules that all people lived by—otherwise a community would just detonate into a million little felons. I'm not sure I disagree. It's a question of who writes the rules, and, as Gracie says, grown-ups are annoying.

25

B ut Gracie's list will have to wait.
"I'm too tired to think," she concludes.
"I'll tape this piece of paper to the fridge and you can
add rules as you think of them."

"And you'll obey?"

"I'll do the best I can." I'm the kind of mother that
launches the great tyrants of world history.

"I'll help you."

"Gracie," I say, "you probably oughtn't to walk around
naked while Grandpa's around."

"Is Grandpa here because Daddy left?"

"No. Coincidence."

"My history teacher says we remake our lives all the time."

"That's true," I nod, just a little jealous that someone else's
life lessons are embossing themselves on my baby.

"She says people get in car crashes or go to war or have
twins or move to Brazil—all the time—and they just have to
remake everything."

"What do you think about that?"

"I'd rather be stuck with the way things were."

My hand rises to my temple and touches a long scar that
slinks into my scalp underneath my hair.

Later in the evening I prepare a sponge bath and some
pudding for Daddy. Each time the pudding spoon touches
Daddy's lips, he opens his mouth. Each time I touch the
straw there, he sips. Daddy has no teeth left (I found them
wrapped in a ball of tissues in the suitcase), so his lips curl
into his mouth.

"Probably all those pork chops, eh, Daddy?" I say.

He used to put the hibachi on the back stoop and cook pork chops into saddle leather. He claimed it was so that we didn't die of trichinosis. Lisa, Claire, and I sat at the kitchen table making gladiator noises. We pretended we were Permian man, trying to pull off pieces of sabertooth tiger meat with our teeth, until our mother shushed us. She said no man married a noisy eater.

I switch on the clock radio so that Daddy can listen for a bit while bathing. It's time for the news. Unfortunately, we are the news: "Houston is battening down for what many people are calling the storm of the century."

"Batten away, eh, Daddy?" I say. I pull the pajamas gently from his old bones. There are wrinkles everywhere. His skin is like liquid until I come to his feet. His toenails are so thick and brittle and translucent, they look like Baltic amber. I fetch my clippers and file and shave them down. Aging wasn't always so cruel. It used to be you could die before the worst started.

"...outer layers of rain just reaching suburbs south of Houston by tomorrow afternoon. NASA says Johnson Space Center is locked down and braced for Category 4 winds. Hurricane Che is spiraling clockwise, bringing heavier rains to the western regions. The brunt of the storm is expected to stall temporarily over Galveston Island, gathering force."

Daddy seems like he is going to shrink steadily until he just disappears with a hushed poof. He already has died, in a way. He's lost any semblance of a life. No physical control. No voice. No vision. I don't think he has twenty-one grams to give up when he passes. I draw fresh pajamas onto his body.

Gracie saunters into the dining room and sits beside me. "Can't sleep," she whispers. She pats her grandfather's leg. "Everybody's decent now, including me," she smiles, pointing to her pajamas. "It smells horrible in here."

"Soap from France. It's called Pamplemousse. French for grapefruit."

"No one really likes grapefruit. That could be our Rule #1 for the refrigerator. Nothing grapefruit."

I tuck Gracie into a grapefruit-free bed and turn out my light. I lie on my back and listen to the night and wonder what will happen to us all. There are times when I desperately crave to know the future. Bobby was mesmerized by the idea that Beowulf was born to be a hero, that his destiny waited for him to emerge from the womb—destiny, like someone patiently smoking a cigarette outside the delivery room door.

Shattering the night's hush is my telephone again.

"It's me!" screams MaryJane. "From gay Paree! I could have danced all night, Julia. Galeries Lafayette threw a huge private party for Pitti Palazzo, and they let me in because I said I was your best friend! I said I came to Paris to evacuate from the hurricane. '*L'orage!*' they said. 'Probably!' I said. Whatever. They don't all speak English! You know, Julia, the French are pretty good about émigrés. At least émigrés dressed like *moi*. I only just got back to the hotel. It was the most incredible party ever. We're going to have to do this in Houston when I get back. Am I slurring my words? Am I speaking Perrier-Jouet? You're a star, Julia!"

A smile falls out of earth's orbit and crashes onto my face. "I'm so flattered, MaryJane."

"Well, I'm going to konk. Good luck tomorrow! Give Gracie a kiss for me. Toodle-heure."

FRIDAY

26

We sleep like the dead, but I wake with a jolt. What if one of us *is* dead! I fly downstairs and reach for Daddy's pulse, which rewards me with a faint drum on my fingertips. Will this be every morning?

Out the window the sky is yellow, going grey. The light seems tentative. Today's the day. No district court of appeals can issue a stay on a hurricane. I pull on some clothes and head up to the attic studio to work with the last hours of electricity. Gracie is at the age where she can register some serious sleep. I finish sewing her school jumper, lowering the hem another inch.

One of my tables was dedicated to a layout of textile swatches and notions. Before the paint. Underneath the table are dozens of boxes that were protected by the plywood. I pull them out. Scrunched in one of the boxes is a baby outfit I made for Sunny Blanton's baby and never gave her—too many buttons. I keep it because I'm not done with the idea, because somewhere in the thread and pleats and corn-yellow Egyptian cotton is a *yes* that the sea of buttons didn't suffocate.

I unpack. Rolls of gimp. Pincushions from Japan and Poland and France. Small baskets of silks from Kanchipuram that diffuse an exotic scent of temple dust and spices. This is my alphabet and my air again. Even the silence is mine. I feel empowered and calm, and I lose the next four hours to my work.

At noon, Gracie needs lunch, plus every blanket and pillow in the house in order to make her hurricane fort. I put the air conditioning to 65 degrees, freshen Daddy, and make him some soup. A strange anxiety creeps into all of us, as though the steady barometric drop were changing the gravity of our molecules. I spend a couple more hours up in my studio finalizing a set of dress designs on paper, while Daddy sleeps and Gracie constructs her fortress. I photograph the designs, scan them, and email them to New York, where the electric grid is safe. At any second our power may decrescendo to a consummate, glassy silence.

The computer blinks hurricane alerts—roads closed, zip codes under compulsory evacuation, gale-force gusts recorded, airport closures. Why were we advised to hunker down? I wonder what was true and untrue about Bobby's summons from Harvard. Was there any Beowulf conference at all? That would be his way, to fabricate his dreams for my illusions, to puff up his scholarly image into a Macy's Thanksgiving Day balloon. Or maybe it was all for Gracie, to tighten the lug nuts of her pride in her father. I feel so sorry for Gracie, compelled by birth to love Bobby and me.

I search for Harvard conferences on the web, and redden with the shame of spying. Our mother spied all the time. She spied through our bedroom keyholes, which was traditional, and she spied on our neighbors, which was cheeky, and she spied on Daddy, which was largely boring until it wasn't. She was an unrepentant spy. Once she took binoculars upstairs and pressed them against my bedroom window to see if she could make out Mrs. Berry's recipe for zucchini bread.

I google Beowulf conferences, but no one on earth right now seems interested in the saga. I google Harvard, click on Events, then Lectures. Nothing about *Beowulf*. It might have been called something else. Something obliquely referring to Old English. I scroll down the list of lectures. There are Gallery Talks on Franz Hals, a symposium on Chinese Business Dynasties, a memorial lecture on Miriam Somebody. There is nothing about English literature, Olde or New(e). I sit back in the chair, trying to figure Bobby's strategy, but my mind never worked the way his did.

A thin fear takes hold of me, drapes like cool silk over my

arms and legs. I want to call Lisa, to talk over the possibilities, but she's got enough on her plate.

"What's the matter?" Gracie says, wandering into the room.

"Nothing. Why?"

"You're humming. You always hum when you're upset. I'm freezing. For lunch, let's have something boiling hot. Emma's mother tried to serve her brussels sprouts once, but Emma threatened to run away from home."

"Only reasonable," I say. "How's the fort?"

"Perfect."

I make us both grilled cheese sandwiches in a panini pan that Bobby, for some reason, never threw.

"You're humming again," Gracie says.

By three o'clock, the air is ugly and morgue-still, but the sky is cloudless. The lights have flickered a few times, suggesting trouble to our south, and I mentally compose a letter to Reliant Energy proposing a corporate name change. Gracie has built an impressive fort in the foyer under an old bridge table. My parents used to have weekly bridge games on this creaky table. The group split up because my mother couldn't tolerate tobacco smoke, and in those days everyone smoked if they breathed. I jam the rickety hinges to keep the table legs from collapsing.

My phone jingles.

It's Lisa. Weeping on the other end.

"They cancelled my promotion," Lisa says. "The Board meets in two days to decide whether to sue me or not."

"What? What happened?"

"I don't know! I was at my desk this afternoon. Two security officers walked in and told me to take my purse, they were going to escort me from the building. Then a third man came in and started putting padlocks on my file cabinets, my desk drawers, even my kitchen cupboards."

"You have a kitchen in your office?"

"A friend in HR said papers came to light that showed I lost the bank five point three billion. I didn't, Julia. I never did that. They won't tell me what these papers are. They won't talk to me. The security guards practically dragged me across the trading floor. They rode the elevator down with me, walked me to the entrance of the building on Sixth Avenue, and stopped. And I just had to keep walking. All New York was watching my humiliation. I could see people filming it with their cell phones. It's the most embarrassing thing that's ever happened to me." She pauses. "Barring Bisskit's outburst during my school play."

"Where are you now?"

"I'm home," she says. She takes deep gulps of air. "I took a Xanax and a Valium. I'm sitting by the telephone. I still have friends there. I'm waiting for information. I think I need just one more Valium."

Lisa has a doctor that prescribes anything she suggests. His office sounds like the Union Square farmer's market of pharmaceuticals, and Lisa can stroll from bin to bin pointing at what she wants.

"What can I do, Lisa?"

"Love me. Believe me."

"I do. Of course I do."

Five p.m. I stare at the phone, waiting for news from Lisa. In the background is the radio streaming Hurricane Che news. Unhappy Freeport took the direct punch and is underwater along with Surfside Beach, Jesús's favorite fishing spot. The outermost muscles of the hurricane are lapping at flat Galveston. Waves are splashing over the sea wall. Forecasters anticipate a twenty-foot tidal surge. If they're right, Galveston is going to take one giant step backward.

I pull Daddy away from the French doors, half underneath the big old table, and I settle an extra quilt on top of him. In a way, I'm glad now that there are no shutters for these old doors. We'll be able to watch the storm from here. There's no telling whether old Mr. Lanier's geckos, or Judge Garwood's grapefruits, or Mimi Blanton's roses will survive. Our foxtail ferns will be pasted to the ground, and the canopy of oaks and pecans will be torn open. Tomorrow morning, if anything is standing, it will be gray with silt and sand and loose filth.

The temperature outside has dropped to eighty-six degrees, nearly pleasant. This afternoon the mayor was apoplectic about Galveston residents refusing to evacuate. The Coast Guard risks their lives to pull idiots from the surf. I try to make a mental list of what I'll miss if Galveston is wiped away. Zip. That was quick.

"Gracie?" I call into the foyer fort. "Any talk about the surge?"

"Nope. It's freezing in here. My teeth are chattering."

We wait, like prisoners, eyes on the noose, ears tuned to the radio. I take a design magazine and a glass of Chardonnay onto the front stoop and watch the condensation bead delicately and race down the stem. Every few minutes I crack open the door and shout into the fort, "News?"

"Nope," Gracie replies. "Unless you live in Surfside. Surfside is gone. And they closed Galveston."

"Closed? Like a shop? How do they close a city?"

"Bomb the bridge?" Gracie offers.

At six o'clock, I realize the first glass of Chardonnay didn't do it—didn't dull the anxiety.

"On its way," Gracie shouts from the fort as I come inside.

"When will we feel it?"

"Around eleven o'clock. If Freeport is zero feet above sea level, how high are we?"

"About fifty feet."

"Can't get us!" she yells triumphantly.

But it's not the water, it's the wind we have to worry about. It's the whip and the punch. I lock the front door and put a second rolled-up towel at its base. The rest of the world is not waiting, like we are—the great hunkered-down—for Che's starter pistol. There is something so lonely about being in a hurricane. You feel like you're in something you cannot measure, left, right, up, down, sixth dimension, eighth dimension, decibels, ohms, energy, mass—and yet, you're inside of it. Although it feels enormous—galactic—most of the planet is oblivious, and most of the country is only mildly curious. You realize you are completely dispensable to the rest of the world.

I head into the kitchen feeling slightly sentimental, as if our last supper is about to begin, and shouldn't it be more grand than fried redfish with roasted potatoes and carrots? Gracie saunters in and gasps when she sees the carrots (profane) next to the potatoes (sacred) at the cutting board (altar).

"No carrots!" she cries out. "Why do you have to ruin dinner?"

"But, Gracie, I love roasted carrots," I say. "You don't have to eat them."

"But I see them." She seizes a disc of cheese coated in red wax and disappears.

Given the overarching stress in the household right now, I'll eat my carrots raw. For the roasting pan, I cut up an onion instead, blotting my eyes with the kitchen towel to staunch the flow of onion tears. Then I toss it into a bowl with the potatoes—nice red fingerling potatoes that look like farmers' fingers, swollen and quirky. Olive oil, sea salt, pepper. Gracie skips back into the kitchen with a big idea radiating across her face. When she sees me, her expression flicks into alarm and anger.

"Why are you crying?"

"Onions," I say.

"Would you just. Stop. Crying? Don't you think this storm is bad enough?" Her voice rises into a scream. "Okay, then roast your stupid carrots!"

I marvel at Gracie's flaming plume of anger. I was never

allowed to express myself that way. Someone or something always interrupted me. Sometimes a smack.

"Onions," I say softly. "Onions would make Attila the Hun tear up. Onions would make an armadillo cry crocodile tears." I collect Gracie in my arms. "And do you know that Bisskit ate a raw onion for lunch every Saturday?"

"Raw?"

"She read in an article that they prevented cancer, and she took it as gospel and ever after there was a bag of onions sitting on the kitchen counter. As I recall, she ate lemon wedges, too, for a while."

"Do they prevent cancer, too?"

"I don't know. But they make you pucker. When we saw Bisskit eating a lemon wedge, our lips twisted into a knot. Your Aunt Lisa brought a lemon wedge to the rodeo parade, and when she bit into it the entire brass section of the marching band collapsed."

"Oh no!"

"Yep."

"Did they put her in jail?"

"Lisa is too clever. She would never get caught."

Gracie is very proud. "I would never get caught either."

Those Calaway girls. We were all crazy, and now we're all unmarried. Lisa has a love-hate relationship with men. Claire has a hate-hate relationship with them. In my mother's day, parents blamed their children for failings. Nowadays, children blame their parents. My eyes flick toward Gracie.

"Should I have dinner in my fort?" she beams. "I could be a pasha in my Arabian tent."

"Do we need to feed all your camels and servants too?"

"No," she says. "I've sent the camels to safety. You can be the servant. I need a towel."

Off she goes to perfect her vision. Already she has commandeered every quilt and blanket in the house to effect her fort, and now it seems she'll be requisitioning the bath towels for her turbans. Towels are a precious commodity during hurricanes. I've rolled several along doors, extra in front of the french doors in the dining room, which are fully an inch off the floor after years of subsidence.

Che is right there, fifty miles to our south, and yet, not a breeze to budge a leaf. I put the vegetables in the oven to slow-roast, and play Go Fish with the pasha in her fort. She has a bath towel wrapped in a spiral on her head. We're both shivering underneath our fleeces.

"Hungry?" I ask after a while.

"Starving, and my turban keeps tipping."

"Want a snack?"

"No."

"Go fish."

"Cheap."

"Do you want to start over?" I say.

"Not yet. Where do you think Daddy is?"

A different kind of cold takes over me. "Boston," I lie.

At seven, the first seashore-scented breezes arrive.

"I'll make dinner now," I say to Gracie.

"I'm not hungry anymore."

"Fried redfish? Your favorite roast potatoes?"

"Can we eat later?"

"Later, we might have to eat it raw."

"Can I watch TV on your laptop in here?" she asks.

"I think that should be Rule #2 on our list," I say. "Before hurricanes, laptops in forts."

I put my head out the kitchen door. The temperature is pleasant. Remarkable is the hush. The birds, who usually mark dusk with their gangland-style racket, are gone or gone mum. I think of the Great Storm of 1900, how the people of Galveston knew a storm was coming, but they had no idea how monstrous it was. The next day 6,000 were dead.

Hurricane Che is throwing out rogue winds over 145 miles per hour. In Freeport. I flash on memories of past storms. Some roared like hours of carpet-bombing. Alicia tore up palm trees and chucked them through the air. She shredded fences and broadcast mud and twigs and turf and oil like a film over the earth. Gas lines burst. Fires exploded in the midst of driving rain. Our whole house shuddered when the Berrys' big live oak flopped over onto our lawn. I'm never cavalier about sitting through a hurricane. You can't anticipate the details of a storm, and at this instant, I wish I'd driven to Austin three days ago.

The first winds spit grit against the window panes. Here we go. Is this what it sounded like inside the Buick, when all the wedding guests hurled their rice? Bisskit said she told them to go home and stop ruining the paint finish.

"It's starting," I call into the fort.

"About time," Gracie says. "I hope I can finish my show before the power goes out."

The phone rings.

"It's me," Lisa says, her voice thick. "They've put my promotion on hold." She bursts into tears again.

"What?"

"Julia, I was never involved in these equity messes."

"I'm sure you weren't."

"They called me at home. The chairman of the Board."

I'm stunned. I don't remember ever hearing Lisa weep. "Sit down," I say. "Have a glass of wine. Lie down a minute." But it turns out my big sister has already polished off a bottle of Cakebread.

"I can't sleep," she says. Then she nearly passes out from a whopping yawn. "Can I call you later?"

"Of course."

"I didn't do it, Julia."

"I know you didn't."

I hang up, only to hear the phone ring.

"Yes?"

"It's me again," Lisa says. "Did the hurricane arrive yet?"

"It's moving into Dodge," I say.

"Are you and Gracie okay?"

"Yes, Lisa. We love you."

"Call me if you need me."

Out the kitchen window, the first loose leaves flutter down from the trees. Oak and pecan branches glance left and right, as though they're looking for an aggressor. Somewhere in the neighborhood, terracotta garden pots just toppled over onto tiled patios. They sound like cowbells. One time we watched a set of garden tools hurtle awkwardly across our yard like tumbleweeds. They got caught in Mimi Blanton's roses. After another storm, Mrs. Berry found all her pool chairs in her swimming pool, so she shocked the pool with cleaning chemicals and the chairs came out gleaming white. Now she does that once a year.

At nine-thirty I poke my head into the pasha's fort. "Dinner in a half hour. Our last hot meal for a while."

I dredge the redfish filets in milk, then flour, then egg, then breadcrumbs. It's how I learned. We were a family of fry cooks. I remember my mother hammering raw slabs of chuck steak into cold, limp flaps of tissue. Men and awls didn't hold a candle to my mother, frowning and pounding, her gritted teeth just visible between two tight lips. She soaked the meat in milk and egg, then in flour, then back in milk and egg, then into breadcrumbs. She dropped a stick of butter into the frying pan and laid each bearded piece of meat into the spitting fat. We ate chicken-fried steak once a week, and there was always something brutal about it. While the meat cooked, my mother Cloroxed the wooden cutting board, a scrap from Roy's crap lumber mill.

27

The lights flicker. Gusts of wind hurl debris against the house. The first salvoes of rain arrive like pellets against the glass.

"Someone knocked on the door," Gracie says, poking her head into the kitchen.

"I hope it's a big bluefish," I say. The butter begins to brown. "Just in time for the frying pan."

"You didn't hear it?"

"I think lots of things are going to knock against our house tonight."

Gracie nods and disappears. Then the knock comes again. Two distinct raps in the middle of storm clatter. I suddenly remember that Dr. Ingram said he'd try to stop by. I turn off the burner and fly to the door. Gracie emerges from her fort with a flashlight. She has hoarded all our flashlights in there and turned off the house lights, the better to realize the value of her merchandise. At ten o'clock she'll open a bazaar.

I flip on the foyer lights expecting to welcome the kindly Ingram. Even in anticipation of his compassionate face and polished bald head, I can feel tears rising up my personal plumbing. Maybe that's what puts him apart from other doctors—the ability to draw water from dry wells.

I pull open the door, already apologizing for my tardy response, and gasp.

It is Claire.

My little-no-more sister, Claire. From back when. She is alarming. Her skin is white and her lips brutishly red and her eyes rimmed in kohl. She stands on the stoop, tall, emaciated, scissored into sharp angles, with pinkish-orangish hair that's pomaded up into golf turf. A chiffon blouse flickers across her bony body as the winds find her. She wears distressed blue jeans and unlaced Converse sneakers with a skull pattern on the canvas. Is it Claire? Maybe it's a third cousin.

"Trick or treat?" the specter says.

It's Claire, all right. It's her voice, deepened over the years by a diet of whiskey and self-immolation. She has our mother's Lladro skin. In fact, Claire has that kind of gaunt perfection that usually results from a professional airbrush.

"May I come in?"

A Gatling gun of cold rain shoots from the dark sky, and Claire cringes under its fire. I take her hand and draw her inside. Locking the door behind her feels strange. It upends the usual scary-outside/safe-inside scenario. The lights flicker again. Gracie and I watch this apparition rub her arms to find warmth. Her fingers are as long as pencils. Very daddy longlegs.

"Claire," I say. I reach out and brush a drop of rain from her cheek. I gently squeeze her shoulder.

Suddenly rain bashes against the house like a wave and we all jump. I might have felt safer on this ship if I hadn't suddenly found Claire on board.

"I came just in time," Claire says.

"Come in," I say. "You must be freezing. Would you like a sweater? Hot tea?" I hear Gracie snort (angelically) at my side (super-glued).

"Great," Claire says. I can see I've amused her. She shakes her head quickly and efficiently, like a dog might, flicking water drops off her pink punk hair. Then her chin lifts, her eyes open wide, and I presume she is inhaling her childhood home. Her eyes scan for clues. Shoe scuff marks, dropped pencil stubs, lost socks.

"The house looks just the same," she says. "You always did like this place."

She speaks with a deeply familiar lilt. The last time I heard it, it was my mother's, and funnily, there was a similar level of indictment wafting through it.

Gracie, who is clinging to me like a starfish on a rock, gives me a thump. People who think God expresses his love in mysterious ways ought to check out children.

"Claire," I say. "I want to introduce you to Gracie."

Claire bends down like a giraffe to investigate. "I am pleased to meet you," she says slowly, inflecting each word with studied form. She vacuums in Gracie's mien.

"Hi," Gracie whispers.

Claire says, the corners of her eyes crimping, "If I had any doubts about coming, they're gone now."

Gracie exhales with delight. "I made a fort," she points (bask, bask).

"Is there room for one more in there?" Claire asks.

Gracie nods.

"But first I'm going to get a cup of tea with your mom. Would you like me to bring you one too?" Claire proposes.

Gracie shakes her head. She looks up at me with big eyes. Aunt Claire must come from a queer country where children are offered bitter grown-up drinks.

I take Claire's hand once more and squeeze it. She looks at me with a flicker of concern, as though she might have gotten into something larger than anticipated. She washes up, then finds me in the kitchen. The dining room is dark. No one would notice Daddy on the floor in there unless he/she snooped.

"You look great," I say, exhaling a short prayer for electricity. "You look beautiful. Wherever you've been, it's been wonderful for you."

"My driver asked if I was going to a costume party," she replies, picking at her blouse. She drifts onto a chair at the kitchen table like a long feather. Her hands reach out and read the piney braille of the old table. Her childhood spent eating meals here. "I won't stay long. I have a room at the Derek."

"You're welcome to stay here, Claire."

"We dropped my things at the hotel. I'm surprised they

didn't fall out of the airplane's cargo hold, given the turbulence. The streets are empty though. That part was easy. Everyone's evacuated. Everyone but you. I promised Hussar I wouldn't be long."

"Hussar?"

"The driver."

"You left someone out there?" I say.

It's pitch-black outside. The winds have begun to wail and rain clatters against the shutters. Soon the thunderheads will boom. It's altogether surreal. And Claire has parked a man in the street.

I glance out the kitchen window, blurry with sheets of rain. Under the streetlights, I can just make out a limousine's orange parking lights. Already the street is a low river.

"I'll run tell him to go," I say. "Maybe it's too late. Maybe he ought to stay with us here."

"It's no big deal," Claire says. "He's in a massive SUV."

"But it's already flooding." Oh, how I hate the sound of my voice. The shade of a scold.

Claire sighs and pulls out her cell phone. "Hussar?" She looks lazily at a business card. "This is Miss Calaway. What does it look like out there? Yes. Yes, I know. Of course." Her eyes become distant while her driver's miniaturized voice shouts passionately. I would love to be that immune to someone shouting at me.

"Right," Claire finally says. "You've got my credit card. My apologies to your family. See you tomorrow." She flicks off the phone. Deep sigh. "I guess if the offer still stands."

"Always."

She is noticeably silent. Maybe life in front of a blank canvas does that.

"It's wonderful to see you, Claire," I say. Small prayer: Please Lord, give me the peace of mind to count my blessings and not faint. Sincerely, Julia Calaway.

Quick blessings inventory. We have lights. We have a gas stovetop to boil water. Gracie isn't running a fever. Bobby is far away. We have food. Maybe there are nine rings of heaven, and Dante meant to explore them, too, but something intervened.

Claire's eyes compute every detail in the kitchen.

"How long has it been?" I ask.

"It feels like yesterday. Where's Bobby?"

"We divorced."

"Thank god. What a bastard."

"Plain to see?"

She nods, looks away, minimizing the revelation of my blindness.

We sip hot smoky tea with cream and sugar. At least, I do. Claire does little more than warm her cheek with the mug. A milk-crust forms on her tea. It's the color of oatmeal, which Claire always hated, no matter how many times our mother served it for breakfast. Claire used to carve images into her oatmeal, before heaving it into the garbage pail.

"I wouldn't feed this to a dog," Claire (post apocalypse) would say.

And my mother would reply, not even turning from the sink. "Good thing we don't have one then."

Does she have a dog now in New York City?

Her eyes examine the kitchen moldings, the cupboard knobs, the floorboards, the tabletop. I cannot imagine the memories triggered by this room. When she was little, Claire would skip across the prairie of our lives with her curls bouncing and her stuffed animals clutched in her arms. "Julia!" she would shout to me with her funny low voice. "My polar bear has a broken arm. You need to sew him a sling."

I'm sure that harrowing memories have quashed any good ones. The injured Claire is the one that sits before me, her identity of bitterness and damage set like concrete.

Claire doesn't speak and I try not to stare at her bony form. I turn to dinner. The redfish filets, cold and hoary grey, look unappetizing. I reheat the butter. The roasted potatoes are warming. I pull the makings of a salad from the refrigerator and set out some cheese and crackers. "You don't have to feed me," Claire says.

Ugh, as Lisa would say. *Odd phraseology*, Bobby might have said. To be fair, Bobby at one time seemed like an antidote to Claire's brand of absinthe.

I can almost hear the thump of our mother's iron against powerless cotton, when Claire would make a stage play of retrieving a single leaf of lettuce from the fridge for lunch.

Claire sits before me now, and all the rage seems like such a waste.

"I was just making dinner," I say to Claire. "There's always enough for one more." She isn't coughing up any smiles so I busy myself with the meal. We're just two stink bugs sharing a flagstone. Maybe she hates me, and hell for her is us sitting together.

"They had dinner on the plane," she says.

Right. I sauté chives and chopped red pepper.

"I don't suppose you have a bottle of wine?" Claire sighs, giving her tea an aggrieved look. She managed to down a gram, or it has evaporated.

"I have wine. And I have bourbon."

"Bourbon. Brilliant. What kind?"

"Knob Creek."

"That'll work. I drink bourbon to reach my alpha state, my painting plane." She has said something personal and stretches like a careful cat.

I try desperately to think of questions for Claire. Do you have a nice studio? Are you working on a new series? Have you got favorite paint colors? Did you get a double mastectomy? "Are you warm enough, Claire?" I ask. "We have extra fleeces."

"It *is* a little like the White Witch's ice palace. But I'll manage."

"Do you remember living through hurricanes?"

A thought crosses her face. I try not to notice.

"No," she says.

"I set the-air conditioning to sixty-five. We'll lose power soon."

"Ah."

"Will you be in Houston long?"

Another flicker in her eyes. "No."

"Have you—"

"Stop. Stop, Julia. It's okay."

"What's okay?"

"Awkwardness. Awkwardness is okay."

I blow back some hairs which tickle my nose. "Right."

"I've come to see him again," she says. "I'm the only one alive now that knows what happened."

"I know he raped you, Claire. It was past horrible. It changed all of our lives."

"There's a lot you were never told."

"I didn't want to intrude. Well, I did, actually, but you didn't let me."

Claire pauses to make a calculation. "There's a lot no one ever knew."

"Claire, you're speaking in runes."

She stiffens and stops speaking altogether. I feel terrible. I know it was unimaginably dire. I have to put the memories in a box each time I tend to Daddy.

I push the vegetables around the pan. They sizzle and pop with reassuring familiarity. I am so grateful for electricity I could weep. Finding Claire on my doorstep with the power out would have put me in the grave.

Claire says, "I always thought that if I told you about the whole event, you would stop loving me."

"I could never stop loving you, Claire."

"You were always the nice one," Claire says. She takes a slug of bourbon. Her eyes narrow. "Hmm."

Gracie skips into the kitchen. "The fort's stocked. I've got food, comics, flashlights—mine is the big one—and pillows. I put in some magic markers and a pad for you, Aunt Claire, in case you want to draw."

Claire observes, "You're nice. Like your mother."

"Aren't you nice?" Gracie asks.

"Nope."

"You're teasing," Gracie says, but nervously.

"*Nyet.*"

Gracie smells a scandal (Claire doesn't make it difficult) and slips onto a chair. Claire turns to me thoughtfully. "Do you still sew?"

I push the wilting vegetables to the edges of the pan and lay down the fish fillets the way I might lay out pieces of appliqué on my worktable. "Yes," I say. "I sew."

"Quilts, clothes, sailboat sails?"

She doesn't even know what I do with my life. She hasn't cared to ask Lisa or to google my name, and she doesn't berate herself for not knowing. I'd like to think *poor Claire*, marooned in my kitchen of normalcy; poor Claire, driven here mercilessly and drowning in painful memories. But instead I think: fuck you, Claire.

I say, "I design clothes."

"Wow. Am I wearing something you designed?"

I shake my head without looking over.

"But I am!" Gracie cries out. She pulls a bowl of grapes from the refrigerator (Oh, ode to electricity, third verse). Gracie marches up to Claire and plucks at her tunic. The fabric is Persian blue cotton with colorful geometric bands running across it helter-skelter. It came from my designs for Pitti's summer collection 2007. Pitti Palazzo saw that families were no longer leaving their children at home. They were vacationing together. We designed a handful of pieces for teenaged girls, and the line sold out immediately. We did a second run for smaller children, and that, too, disappeared. At which point Pitti Palazzo terminated the project. "No more," the Italians said. "Or they'll be knocking down our doors!" Maybe fanatical consumerism was a bad thing in Rome. The American contingent was left scratching its head.

"Wow," Claire says, this time softly, and with a hint of

rusty candor. She fingers the fabric and surveys the cut. Claire is probably the type of psychotic who could appreciate well-placed darts.

Gracie says, "My mom is Pitti Palazzo, and she's going to do girls' clothes next."

"Pitti Palazzo. Lisa didn't tell me," Claire says. "Or maybe she did and I forgot."

"How is Lisa?" I ask, testing.

"Lisa is fine. She was born fine."

I flip the fish and set out slices of sweet peppers for Gracie. Suddenly the kitchen is full of cheerful noises. Gracie's crunching and the sizzling fish beat away the loud battering of rain.

"I need a piece of ice for this," Claire declares, rising up with her bourbon. "To slow me down." She opens the freezer, which is empty, save for the ice cube trays. "Lucky that's all I wanted."

Has she forgotten? The power may be out for days. "We eat out of the freezer beforehand, don't we, Gracie?"

"Frozen waffles," Gracie says. "Frozen bagels, ice cream, popsicles, chicken nuggets, and a frozen pizza that stank."

"You ate it all."

"I was starving. Starving people will even eat each other!"

Claire looks over. "Good, then, to have a pizza around." She takes a gulp of chilled bourbon and then a deep breath. "So, where is he?"

28

Claire stands in the doorway of the dining room for a long time. She says nothing. I leave her be. I don't want to stand too close to Claire. I might hear incantations.

Gracie and I have dinner alone.

"What does *nyet* mean?" Gracie whispers.

"It means nope."

"That's what I guessed."

We put on KTRH and learn that Che is gaining strength. Trees are dropping in Pearland, ten miles down the road. Power is spotty. Winds are blasting the glass out of office buildings. Yes, yes, I think. This hurricane is getting boring and it's only just arrived. My thoughts return to Lisa, stripped of her lofty banking stripes, sitting alone in her swanky Manhattan apartment, tears splashing into her wine. Four times I call. Four times I'm diverted to her answering machine. When my phone rings, I grab it straightaway. I want her to know I'm here for her, and I want to tell her who else is here.

"What's happening?" I ask breathlessly.

"I'm terribly sorry, Miss Calaway. I'm running late. Hospice attempted a late evacuation and several patients passed."

"Dr. Ingram! I thought it was my sister calling. Doctor, you do not have to stop by tonight. You mustn't come by. It's too dangerous."

"Kind of you to say, Miss Calaway. But I'm almost at your house. I just wanted to let you know I didn't forget you. I have your father's file."

"You're making me cry again, Dr. Ingram."

"Crying is normal in situations like these," he says, very doctor-ish.

I hear the plash of his tires plowing through high water. I picture his little form clinging to the steering wheel, navigating toward where the middle of the road is supposed to be.

"But your family," I say, imagining a perfect quartet of little Ingrams.

"I'm divorced, Miss Calaway. I'm afraid being a doctor made me a substandard husband. That's what I was told, anyway." There was another high-water *whoooosh* on the line. "I'll just—Oh dear—"

A meaningful *clunk* on his end. Then nothing.

"Okay," I say to no one. "Hello? Hello?"

I put down the phone and run to the front door and swing it open, hoping I'll be able to find him. A wall of rain slaps me backward, drenches me in a split second with cold, cold wet. It is impossible to see in the darkness. The light from our foyer flickers off the sheets of water. I slam the door shut and towel off.

Maybe Ingram won't be coming after all. I could tell him what really makes a substandard husband. My fingers reach up to my temple. The scar is bumpy, like poorly sewn suede. I remember that evening, and the way Bobby's hand swung out of the air like an apparition. It reminded me of roaches; they skate across the floor like darts, and you see them out of the corner of your eye and you think maybe you've got peripheral neuropathy.

Claire's voice interrupts.

"Your phone is ringing."

"Thank you." I pick up. "Hello?"

"Ohmygod!" Lisa cries out. "I thought you weren't there!"

"Speak louder."

"Julia, I can't stop crying. I'm just sick. I've gone gray in the last two hours. By tomorrow I'll look like Bella Abzug."

"Never!"

"I couldn't sleep, so I took some uppers to help me stay focused."

"How about two liters of water," I say.

"How's Daddy? I'm going to come to Houston. I'm going to help you with this. It will distract me."

"You can't fly to Houston. You've got too much to do there. Oh, and we're in the middle of a hurricane."

"Sounds like! There's a ton of static on the line. I can charter a jet," she says. "They fly into tornadoes if you pay them."

"Lisa, you've been framed. You need to stay there get to the bottom of this."

"It's Hadges, Julia."

"I wondered."

"Do I call him? Confront him?"

"I don't know."

"I could sue him."

"For what?"

"It might flush him out of hiding," Lisa says. "Wait! There's a call on the other line. I'll call you right back."

"I'll be here." That's for sure.

At that moment there's a knock on the front door. I sprint to it, passing Claire, who hovers ghoulishy in the dining room doorway. I throw open the door to find a completely drenched Dr. Ingram.

Under the foyer light, he looks like a drowned possum. He glistens with wet. His glasses are hanging off one ear, and a pool of water is darkening under his feet. He seems momentarily disoriented. That's when I notice the name embroidered on his white lab coat: Dr. Mary Obalu. He smiles weakly, then turns his head. A big gash on his forehead sparkles under the chandelier. Bright red blood streams down his cheek.

I pull Ingram into the kitchen and wrap him in dry towels. His eyes flick toward the dining room, where he may have caught a glimpse of something summoned at a séance.

"Would you like a bathrobe?" I ask. "I could put your things into the dryer."

"I'm fine. I was lucky to be wearing a hat," he says.

I make an agreeable noise. No hat.

"What happened?" I ask. My voice is nearly drowned in a howl of wind and rain. I wet a clean dishtowel and daub at his gash. It is four inches long and looks like someone has used pinking shears. "You need stitches, Dr. Ingram."

"The curbs are underwater," he says. "I couldn't make out the contours of the street, and I never saw the hydrant."

It takes only six inches of flowing water to sweep away a car, only three inches to sweep away a person. I pull out a cookie tin that has our first aid supplies. Gracie decorated it with a big red cross, which I told her would get her over any international border. She then went on to embellish the sides with skulls and crossbones, which I told her was her ticket to Somalia. The mixed message isn't lost on Ingram.

"Your survival rate looks dangerously close to ours at hospice," he says.

Gracie saunters into the kitchen aiming her searchlight at him.

"You're our second patient," she chirps, clicking off her light.

"Hydrogen peroxide," I say, showing Ingram the bottle.

"It's gonna hurt," Gracie says reliably.

Ingram laughs quietly. "You're very good to warn me." He swallows a flash of pain. An expression of deep weariness overwhelms him. "I'm not accustomed to being the patient." He flinches as I clean the wound. The hydrogen peroxide makes everything fizzle white. Then out pulses fresh black blood. I try to pinch the skin together with gauze and tape.

Gracie whispers, "Are we going to put Dr. Ingram in the dining room too, Mama?"

"The storm stalled over Galveston," Ingram says. "I thought I'd have time to drive here."

"Che is two hundred miles across," I say. He must be from

not-Texas. "It could be stalled over Beaumont and you still shouldn't be on the roads."

A little Neosporin. A jerry-rigged butterfly bandage. There's too much blood. I work as efficiently as I can while we listen to the storm. It's been a long time since I touched a man, besides Daddy, the fractional man.

"Hold your hand on this, Dr. Ingram. You have to apply pressure."

"You make a very good nurse, Miss Calaway. I apologize for arriving in this state. Let's take a look at your father. Then I need to get back to hospice."

Cut. Why is everyone behaving so ridiculously? The kitchen lights blink, reminding me how many warnings you get in life before you have to make a good decision.

"You're not leaving in this storm, Dr. Ingram," I say. In reflex, I clap my hands over my mouth. Declarative sentences aren't my strong point.

Gracie gives me a big eye roll.

Ingram takes a breath and holds it, thinking, or maybe bracing against the pain. He holds his breath so long I think I'll die watching.

Rain screams against the house. The little pig with the brick house didn't know about hurricanes that dissolve your mortar. Sitting out hurricanes is like sitting out the siege of the Alamo. Noble you. RIP.

"Miss Calaway," Ingram finally says. "Might I trouble you for a glass of whiskey?"

"Bourbon?"

"Perfect, thanks."

"You've had a terrible day," I say.

"The emergency generators at the hospice facility are in the basement, the first area to flood. This is exactly what happened during Tropical Storm Allison, but hospice hasn't had the funds to renovate. Already eight patients have died." His phone, clipped to his belt, beeps. As he reads his message, I get the bourbon.

"Thank you," Ingram says.

Claire wanders into the kitchen like a comfortable wraith. I top up her glass, which has become one with her fingers, and pour one for myself.

"You're my father's doctor," Claire says. She has to raise her voice to be heard above the storm.

"What? Oh yes, I am," Ingram says. He turns to me. "The third Calaway daughter?"

"This is Claire," I say, by way of inelegant introduction.

"So, how is he?" Claire asks Ingram.

Ingram looks at Claire with discernment, and then shrugs. "He's dying, Miss Calaway."

"I suppose you've taken his history."

"I don't have the luxury of chatting with many of my patients," he says. "That's the misfortune of late-geriatric medicine."

"But you've read his file," Claire says.

"Top to bottom."

"What do you think?" This is clearly a coded line of questioning. Ingram hesitates, so Claire goes on. "I mean, a man on so many medications. What is him and what is the drugs?"

"Yes. I think I know what you're asking me."

"How much of his behavior," Claire taps out, "was he really responsible for?"

Ingram takes a thoughtful slug of bourbon. "Your father taught history at St. John's School for over thirty years. That indicates a meaningful control over his actions."

Claire flushes. Did she want it all to have been temporary insanity? Ingram's judgment cuts to her bones. He adds, "My impression is that people do the best they can in life. With life. Many people with great accreditation believe me to be wrong."

"How very circumspect," Claire says.

"People are more limited than we like to believe," Ingram says. "I can't imagine how one apologizes for that. We are, to a large degree, a bucket of chemicals. Not every bucket is stable. Actually, very few are." Claire is as still as a column. "You have a quandary, Miss Calaway," the doctor says, blanketing his intelligence with compassion. "What happened to you was not the crime of a fully competent man."

"My mother wouldn't press charges," Claire hisses.

I put a hand on Claire, feel the tissue-thin fabric of her blouse and the rigid tension of her body. When she doesn't shake me off, I think I'll pass out with happiness. Claire is letting me touch her! All these years later. Claire is not sending me away.

"Do you live in Houston, Miss Calaway?" Ingram asks.

"Nein," she says. In Claire's world, children drink hot bitter tea and learn 150 ways of saying No. "Sorry about your head," she adds to Ingram. Then she gives a theatrical inhalation and drifts out of the kitchen.

Ingram observes her long enough to take in the cell count and breast count.

29

My cell phone beeps.

"I'm back," Lisa shouts. Her head sounds clear. "I've got an idea what happened. All roads lead back to a group in unsecured credits. The CPOs. They bought bundles of—"

"Lisa, Dr. Ingram's just come to check on Daddy. He's bleeding and drenched and—"

"Ooh! Let me say hi," Lisa says.

"My sister, Lisa, would like to say hello," I say, handing the phone to Ingram. We're in the hallway with its little bar area. The night is young, so I root around for more bourbon. I nearly burst into song when my hand lands on a bottle of scotch whiskey in the back of the cupboard and another of Knob Creek. How to be your own best friend.

"Miss Calaway," Ingram says to Lisa. "How are you?"

I hear Lisa's voice buzz. Ingram holds the phone with one hand and presses the gauze against his forehead with the other. In spite of my bandages, blood continues to ooze.

"That's what I've heard," Ingram says. "Yes. That's the story. I don't know yet. I just arrived. Tell me again, please? Yes. Yes. Okay, I'll hand you over."

Ingram gives me the phone. What I hear is, "Wait, I need to ask him something else." I hand the phone back.

He listens. "It's just a small cut," he says. He pulls the gauze away from his head. It's completely soaked with bright red blood. I worry he's going to faint. Instead, he slaps the wet compress back against his head. But the compress, now a sodden peat of fresh blood, squirts (explodes) across his face, his shirt, the phone, his bourbon—everywhere.

"Oh, damn," Ingram says, and drops the phone.

Lisa's voice is on the floor screaming, "What happened? What the hell happened?"

"I'm so sorry," says Ingram. His face is lacquered with blood. He's got the guilty gauze in his hand. It is saturated and dripping through his fingers. He looks at it with profound exhaustion.

And then he faints. *Bonf!* He crumples into a heap on the floor.

"No!" I cry out.

I pick up the phone lying next to him on the wood. "Lisa?"

"Are you okay?" she shouts from Manhattan, where there is no driving rain, no screaming winds, no swooning doctors, no scary Claires.

"Fine," I say. She knows perfectly well it's a bold-faced lie.

"Who dropped the phone?"

"Don't take it personally."

We are apparently causing enough of a commotion to rouse Claire from her favorite doorway. She peruses the scene. Then she kneels down and examines the spatter of blood.

"I wonder if I could paint with this before it dries," she muses.

I experience a paroxysm of revulsion. Lisa's voice comes over the wires again. "What? Hello? Who's there?"

"Claire's here," I say.

A very, very strange yowl erupts from the Manhattan end of the line. Gracie's little form appears in the hallway. She spots a prone Dr. Ingram and utters a soft, "Uh-oh."

I thrust the phone at her. "Gracie, can you talk to Aunt Lisa a sec?"

Gracie snatches the phone and disappears into her fort.

I glance quickly at Claire, who's dipping one spindly index finger into a bead of blood and sniffing it. A weird noise is trying to escape my throat. I drag Ingram back into the kitchen. Far be it for me to notice that Claire not once offers to help. And yet, I have to pinch myself. I don't know who

Claire is, not anymore, not since I was sixteen. We are no longer "in it together." We are as independently configured as two bolts of fabric. My love is unilateral. This is not a reunion.

It would have been easier to grab Ingram by the feet, but I can't bring myself to do it. I put a towel under his head, get my hands under his armpits, and fishtail my way into the kitchen. His head lolls left and right and my house looks like a movie set for *The Texas Chainsaw Massacre*. Not to mention, my bonkers sister wants to make a mural with his blood. I have half a mind to open the front door and let Hurricane Che blow the Gulf of Mexico through my house. If Ingram were conscious, I wouldn't blame him for running hell-bent out the door.

"Hi there," I say, sounding eminently deranged.

"What is your emergency?"

I explain the situation.

"We have all emergency vehicles currently in service," the woman says. "I'm going to patch you through to triage."

I'm on the landline, while Gracie recounts the worst to Lisa on my cellphone. Ingram is spread-eagle on the kitchen floor with towels under his head and a new makeshift butterfly bandage on his forehead. Whoever Dr. Mary Obalu is, she's out a lab coat. I ripped several ribbons out of it to wrap around Ingram's head.

The triage nurse comes on the line, giving her name so fast I never hear it.

"Do you need to know who I am?" I ask.

"No."

Something about her certainty hits me like a two-by-four. "Our doctor was driving over and hit a hydrant in the water. He arrived with a four-inch gash on his forehead, diagonal across his temple, and it won't stop bleeding. He passed out, but he's breathing. Yes. I tried that. Yes, you can kind of pinch the skin together. I understand. Tilted upright. And what? Say again? Are you serious?"

Gracie ambles in, chatting amiably to Lisa. "No, he's on the floor. His eyes are closed but his mouth is open," she reports. "Here's Mama."

Gracie whispers quickly to me, "What's a morgue?"

I switch phones. "Lisa," I say.

"You sound stoned," she says.

"All I said was hello."

"Gracie told me Auntie Claire is drawing flowers on the walls with Dr. Ingram's blood."

"At least she's not drinking it," I say.

"Are you going to call an ambulance?"

"They're completely tied up," I say. "That is a factoid."

"Factoid? You are stoned."

"Lisa, I just spoke with a triage nurse and she said I had to sterilize a needle and try to stitch up Ingram."

"You are shitting me!"

"The gash is too long and too deep to bandage," I say. "And I can't get him to the ER. Lisa, the hurricane is on top of us, right now."

"I gather. And you can stop shouting. It's nice and quiet on my end. Why didn't you evacuate, anyway?"

"They said it wouldn't be too bad."

"Well, I'm watching it on my TV and I can promise you it's the biggest hurricane I've ever seen in my life."

"And then Daddy arrived."

"I told you he's a blindside tackle."

"I'm going to sterilize a needle in boiling water," I say. "And I'm going to finish my bourbon, and then I'm going to sew."

"You're the seamstress," Lisa says. "Sounds like you're underneath a freight train."

"I know everything about sewing, right?" The lights flicker.

"Skip the pleats," Lisa says. "And no buttons or zippers. I can't believe I'm missing this."

"Talk to me, Lisa, while I pull myself together."

I raise the doctor's head on blankets I scavenge. We're running low, given Daddy, the pasha's fort, and Claire. I choose thin, steel needles from my tailor's satchel and boil them.

After five minutes, I drain the needles on paper toweling in a colander. I pretend not to notice that Ingram's blood has been finger painted into ornate floral designs by the bar. I do appreciate that Claire has chosen peonies in lieu of her usual cadaverous images. While I'm sipping bourbon to calm my stomach, Lisa fills me in on the newest details of her scandal.

It was Hadges. "Since 2010, Silverman-Shaw had a small backroom division dabbling in equities," Lisa says. "They thought they were buying at the very bottom of the market, they thought they could be like hedge funds, and they thought they were smarter than everyone else. But then the Feds enacted new capitalization laws and this group suddenly had to get the securities off their books. But they couldn't. They actually bought more, thinking it would be a better product if they bundled it up with other things, like school loans. And a year later Silverman-Shaw found itself owning billions in unsecured equities."

"Say again? In English? Ouch."

"What happened?"

"I don't usually sew with blistering hot needles. Go on, Lisa, before I lose my bourbon-buzz."

I have never felt suspended in my own disbelief before. I put the receiver on the floor and set it to speakerphone. Ingram is about to be stitched together like a ripped seam. His skin is so soft. I pinch it together and poke. There's no resistance, although it pulls gently at my thread. Bourbon alone stops my stomach from flipping.

"You can't sew him if you're drunk, Julia. Try a paper clip."

"Talk, Lisa," I say. At that instant, the house shivers from a massive gust of wind. "And talk loudly."

"It started back with Bush and got worse under Obama. The government encouraged banks to get back into the market, to get the country on its feet after the mortgage crisis. High-risk borrowing was back, only under a different name."

"I'm with you."

"Better if you're with the doc, Julia."

"Keep talking."

"The Fed kept rates ridiculously low to encourage lending after the crisis. The worry was, if there's another financial crisis, you have no tools left in your toolbox. You can't drop interest rates when they're just hovering above zero."

"Wow," I say. I realize I ought not to have used white cotton thread. It was Swiss, so I figured it was the most hygienic, which is probably racial profiling. I keep sewing while Lisa's voice sings out from my phone. I don't understand the half of what she's describing. She pauses.

"I didn't do it, Julia," she says.

"I know you didn't. Of course you didn't. Ugh—" I drop the blood-slick needle. My stomach gives a warning heave.

"Remember the Civil War and the power of whiskey!" Lisa shouts out.

"And systemic shock."

"I can't believe you've still got power."

"Me neither."

I wash my hands and pick up a new needle from the colander. Sweet Dr. Ingram is going to come out of this hurricane looking like he tried to catch falling panes of glass.

"He just keeps bleeding," I say to Lisa.

"Can you cauterize the area with a match?"

"The right side of his face?"

"Wait, Julia. I'm googling sutures. You need a tissue forceps to hold the skin together."

"A what?"

"Forget it. The photos are horrible. Let's talk about the weather. Or maybe not."

I sew two stitches. The skin makes me marvel. It swells around the stitches to dam the blood.

"Do you remember MaryJane?" I say. "She's my friend from high school. She picked up Gracie one night when you were here."

"She was wearing more gold than most countries have in their reserves."

"MaryJane evacuated to Paris," I say.

"MaryJane could afford to pay God to blow Che toward New Orleans."

Lisa's calm voice wafts into my ears. She tells me about the documents that Proctor Hadges would have had access to, and which might put her near the group that made the bad investments.

"The really big news is that Bennet Brothers may dissolve this weekend," she says in hushed tones. "We weren't the only bank investing in garbage."

"I can't hear you."

"Are you almost done?" she shouts. "Wait. Don't tell me yet. I have to open another bottle of wine. I think I'll make it bubbly. I'll be right back."

Claire ambles into the kitchen. Nice girl. After all that finger painting, she has neglected to wash her long fingers. She reviews them under the kitchen lights the way Texas women review their manicures.

"Is it always so exciting here?" she says.

Was that a joke? Is she trying to be kind?

"Did I leave my glass in here?" she wonders.

"I don't remember."

"You're sewing," she notices.

"Yeah."

"Kind of ironic."

Lisa would laugh, but Claire is light years away from laughter.

I have less than two inches done. Outer poke left, interior poke right, tie off. Daub clean. His skin surrenders and obeys. Cotton with 6 percent Lycra. Probably as hygienic as a barn.

"Claire," I say. "Can you look after Gracie for me?"

"Sure. Shall I take her for a walk around the block?"

I pause.

"I was joking," she says.

Maybe that's Lower West Side humor. I say, "Actually, do you think you could persuade her into a warm shower before the power goes off?"

Claire drifts away. I take it for a *Yes, sure, my pleasure, anything I can do to help!*

Lisa comes back on the line. "Almost done?"

I put her on speakerphone. "He's coming to, Lisa. Dr. Ingram? Don't move your head."

"Club him!" Lisa calls out helpfully.

Ingram moans. He winces as his brain mounts its trench into a fire storm of consciousness. His eyes cut sharply to the right, where my knots are.

"Sorry," I say.

"You, Miss Calaway, are a very brave woman," he says. "Don't let me interrupt."

"Yay, Julia!" hoots Lisa.

The doctor turns his face, making his wound more accessible. He closes his eyes. "If you don't mind, I won't watch."

"The triage nurse said you needed stitches," I say.

"Is your sister the triage nurse?" he asks. His voice wavers.

"911. That triage nurse."

"Also good," he says.

"I would have told her the same thing," Lisa calls out.

I say, "I boiled everything first. You won't die of infection. Not tonight anyway."

"So smart of you."

"Do you want some aspirin?" I ask.

"No aspirin!" Lisa yells. "It's a blood thinner. Am I on speakerphone?"

"Aspirin impedes clotting," the doctor agrees. "Do you have any Motrin?"

"I do. Will you hold my needle one sec?"

Ingram looks at my needle curiously. "What kind of needle is this?"

"It's a carbon steel milliner's needle, very small gauge."

"You're a milliner?" he asks.

"A clothing designer."

Lisa shouts, "Three cheers for my little sister!"

I gesture to the phone. "Lisa has been assisting with the surgery."

"You Calaway women have many skills," he says.

Lisa yells, "Don't let her play the clarinet for you, Doc!"

I help him wash down several tablets with water.

"Lisa," I say, returning to my sewing. "How did you know aspirin stops your blood from clotting?"

"Everybody knows that," Lisa says. "Everybody's taking a baby aspirin a day now. For their hearts, isn't it?"

"Yes," says Ingram.

"Should I take aspirin?" Lisa calls out.

"Is that the only pill you have left?" I ask her.

"Half a baby aspirin won't hurt," Ingram says. He inhales deeply, reminding me of the Lamaze method of useless diversion.

Soon Lisa has Ingram in a verbal armlock discussing the merits of antidepressants, and I'm about to finish the last few stitches when Gracie's voice booms down the stairs. "Aunt Claire said you said I need to shower!"

I pull back from the doctor's ear. "It's a good idea before the power goes off."

"Repent!" Stomp stomp stomp. Nonetheless, I hear water gurgle through the pipes.

"What time is it?" Ingram asks, flinching each time I poke his skin.

Lisa says, "About one. East Coast time."

"Midnight," I say. "The storm is bearing down now."

"You must know the mayor," the doctor says. "You have electricity."

Lisa's voice, "She has what?"

"Electricity!" I shout.

"Her wires are buried," Lisa shouts back. "Guys, I have to put the phone down a sec. Faxes are pouring in. Don't go away."

I sigh without thinking, and the third needle drops. The lights flicker again (*no-no-no-no-no-no-no-no-no!*), and then go out.

"Hold on," I say to the helpless, prone Ingram. "I'll get the battery lamp. I'm almost done. I have ice for you to apply when it's over."

"Ice," he smiles. "Thank goodness for ice."

My cell phone rings. Lisa.

"Did you lose power?" she says. "Your landline just went out."

"Yes. I'm looking for the Coleman lantern now."

"You are absolutely shitting me."

"Colemans run on batteries these days."

"Even so."

I finish sewing up Ingram under dim battery light, while Lisa kindly reads the *New York Times* to us ("Do you want to hear about water quality, irredeemable foster kids, or the Browns trading their running back to the Colts?" "Dr. Ingram?" "Water quality, please."). Ingram's blood gradually becomes content to rest behind my stitches, and we're all impressed about the level of bacteria in the Hudson River.

Finally, "Done," I say. "Rest. Are you cold?"

"No, no," he says, but he's shivering and sounds like he's going to faint again.

Lisa's voice, "Are you done? God that was boring! Everybody knows the Hudson is filthy."

I steal some blankets off Gracie's fort. As if she knows, Gracie wails from her shower. "No hot water! SOS! I still have shampoo in my hair! Call the Coast Guard!"

I tuck the blankets around Ingram. People look so different lying on their backs, gravity making tiny revisions to the way their skin hangs off their bones. I lie down beside him on the kitchen floor, wishing my glass of bourbon were nearby.

Lisa's voice rings out, "What are we doing next?"

30

One p.m. The true brunt of Hurricane Che moves onto Houston, releasing water in torrential sheets and gusting 145-mph winds. I can feel it on top of us. The house shudders. The shutters rattle. The pounding rain is deafening. Daddy, in the dining room, is the only quiet thing. Gracie has fallen asleep in her fort. I help Ingram to the living room couch, where he sits like a cadaver. He keeps his eyes shut, but he doesn't sleep. His cell phone beeps every few minutes.

There's a drip, drip, drip in the fireplace. I stick a glass under it. The battery-operated radio plays softly on the coffee table. Che is swirling over Houston (*static crackle crackle*). I sit by the front windows, chatting with Lisa, who is watching television coverage of the storm from New York.

Claire, having haunted the upstairs for a while, walks into the living room.

"Is that Lisa?" Claire asks, pointing to the phone in my ear. I nod. She notices the glass in the fireplace. "Glass half full," she says. Queen of Comedy. She saunters back through the dark to the dining room.

The heavy outside shutters tip just enough for me to glimpse swirling sheets of water whipping through the air villainously. Branches and leaves are rocketing everywhere like missiles.

"Lisa," I say. "It's late. You need to sleep so that you can think straight in the morning."

"You don't want my company?"

"I love your company, but it's late here, too, and I may try to sleep."

"Did Gracie go to sleep?" she asks.

"In her fort."

"I love that baby," Lisa sighs.

"I feel like I need to hire someone to protect her."

"From you or from Bobby?"

"Funny. Hey, you never told me: how did you know Bobby had been in the house?"

Lisa clears her throat, which is always a disquieting sign. "I hired a PI in Houston to follow Bobby. I was worried about you. He calls me once a week unless there's an emergency or Bobby leaves town. He's the one that called to say Bobby was in your house. He neglected to mention the paint cans. I had to chew him out."

"I can't believe this."

"Julia, Bobby is a garden-variety maniac. I don't want him to burn down the house. The court won't put him away if you don't have evidence. Anyway, the PI's a sweetie. His name is Naldo and he's got gout. He says surveillance is a bitch."

Mechanically, I look out toward the street, which is a roiling Gulf tributary. My house is shorefront property.

"Gout?" I say.

"In his big toe," Lisa says. "Apparently really painful."

I take the phone from my ear. "Dr. Ingram, what do people do for gout?"

"Anti-inflammatories," he replies, never opening his eyes, hardly opening his mouth. "Glucocorticoids. A quick course of prednisone wouldn't hurt."

"Did you hear that, Lisa?" I say.

"I'll tell Naldo-lito," she says. "He evacuated his family to Monterrey, but he'll be back after the hurricane. Julia, I have got to get some sleep. I'll call you in the morning, okay? See how you weathered the storm. Is the house still cool?"

"Freezing."

"Good sleeping."

"Lisa," I whisper. "Claire says there's lots I don't know about what happened. You know, I've always thought there was something I hadn't been told."

"I know," Lisa says. "I know what you mean."

There's a loud crack outside. My shoulders spontaneously hunch. Ingram's eyes open.

"I try to go back over it sometimes," Lisa reflects. "Daddy whisked away to The Clinic. Mother always taking Claire to new doctors. Suddenly boarding school. And then I was gone. When I've approached Claire, she promises me I don't know the half of it. She says that over and over. Then Claire became someone else, and who's to say she wouldn't have changed anyway? I mean, time reshapes people in odd ways. Look at Bobby. He didn't give a lot of clues in the beginning that he was a psychopath."

We say goodnight. My cell phone battery is low. Tomorrow I'll charge it in the car. This is the time of night when people who don't believe in ghosts entertain eerie superstitions. The house is weirdly still without electrons racing through the wires. Outside is an ion apocalypse.

"Does Lisa have gout?" Ingram suddenly pipes up from the couch.

"No," I say. "Her PI."

"Ah." He's silent for a minute. "My wife hired a private investigator when she decided to divorce me. He followed me everywhere. I treated his deep vein thrombosis. Too many stationary hours in that profession. It leads to several afflictions."

"You took your Hippocratic oath seriously," I say, with a smile.

"Oh, I'm colder and less compassionate than you think," he says.

"I can't believe that." I think of all the times we found him tearing up among bereaved family members at hospice. I pull the cashmere throw from the back of the couch and cover him.

"I promise you I won't testify against your sister," he says.

I go all swimmy-headed. "What do you mean?"

"It's easy to see she's come to even a terrible score. I had time to review the whole file. It's impossible to understand why they didn't put your father in prison. Well, but times were different. Your mother refused to press charges."

"Claire was the victim of both her parents."

"What was your mother to do, really?" he considers. "Three daughters to raise. She needed the income. I can't imagine how Claire survived it all."

"She didn't," I say.

The glass in the fireplace is full. I walk to the kitchen for a bucket. There is a loud swish and a thump. I look out the window but can't quite make out what I'm seeing.

And then I realize. It's a mass of palm fronds. The Phoenix palm. It's fallen against the house.

I put the bucket in the fireplace. I replace the damp beach towels rolled up at the foot of the doors and throw them on top of the dryer. I check the blankets over Gracie, Daddy, and Ingram. Then I head upstairs and find Claire in the guest room, in her clothes, under a sheet. She's staring at the ceiling like a vampire.

"Are you comfortable?" I ask, sitting down on the side of her bed.

"Entirely."

"Can you sleep?"

"I never know."

We listen to the winds ram rain against the shutters. How many times, as children, had we bundled up to wait out a hurricane? We would gather under Lisa's bed and tell ghost stories, compare arm hair, betray secrets.

"Do you remember how Lisa hated the hair on her arms?" I say.

"Vividly," Claire says.

"She used to cry after waxing. So painful. And then, as soon as a hair started growing back, she tweezed. Bleached. Shaved. She was so obsessed with hair."

"Still is."

"Do you see her?"

"No," Claire says abruptly. Then, "She comes to my open-ings."

"She flew to Japan for one, didn't she?"

"So?"

"Nothing. I just remember her saying." I sigh. "You're an international phenomenon. It's great."

"I suppose."

"I'm glad you've come, Claire. I'll see you in the morning."

The skinny upstairs hallway feels like a long country mile. At every step I hear the sound of three girls laughing, fighting, teasing, comforting, plotting, learning, comparing, and adjusting. This matted carpet must be full of traces of our growing up. Lisa still swears she lost an earring in the pile. In this hall we had little flea markets, cleaning the junk from our drawers and trading it for a sister's junk. This hall was our Westheimer Road, our private artery, our route to safety from the outside world, our collective spinal cord. Until Daddy found the door through and brought violence.

I turn around and tiptoe back to the guest room.

"Claire?" I whisper.

"No," she says. "Don't."

I sleep fitfully, roused by the scream of a gust of wind, or a branch launched against the house. I flip over. I think I hear Claire pacing the guest room. I dream of a house on fire. The flames lick, pop, and crackle. I keep running inside it and dragging people out to safety. Then someone cries out, *He's still in there!* and I run back through the flames.

I wake up anxious and sweating. Someone in the tiny hours of morning has put a quilt over me. I can't imagine who, although it's very, very easy to cross the possibilities off my list.

I push the quilt off. The hurricane is heaving its water onto the house. There's no thunder, only the rain and high-pitched screaming of wind. I'm suddenly conscious of another noise downstairs. There is a slap, then enraged whispered words, then another slap. I stumble out of my bedroom. The guest room is empty. I fly downstairs. Gracie is safely asleep in her fort. In the living room, Ingram tries to get up from the couch.

Claire is on Daddy's mattress. She kneels on top of him, cursing him, spitting out volumes of loathing. I've never heard her talk so much. Then she slaps him, again, hard across the face.

Just like Bobby used to do to me.

I throw myself on Claire, pulling her away from Daddy.

"Stop it," I say. She's strong for a science closet skeleton. Her forearms feel like thin iron pipes.

"Let go of me, Julia. You don't know. The bastard. The fucking bastard. It's going to end now." She rips herself from my arms and crawls back to Daddy with a fist raised.

I launch myself into her, toppling her off the mattress.

"Don't make me hurt you, Julia," she grunts.

"There's nothing left of him, Claire."

"It is justified!"

"That's not even Daddy anymore."

"You don't know!"

"Then tell me!" I say fiercely. A fury blisters through me. I rage against thirty years of Claire's desertion. I rage against every guarded pain that walks the earth. I have an impulse to Mirandize her.

She pauses, heaving, lets me think she's considering a profound revelation. Then, "Someone is outside," she says. We're on the floor by the french doors.

"Try to stay on message," I say.

"Get off me already, Julia."

I fall back. "Why not call Hussar?" I say. "He'll be here in a few hours. You could go get some sleep."

But she's strangely distracted. "You've got a prowler."

I'm beyond sense. Bourbon and exhaustion have flooded my veins. I'm going to pass out on the floorboards.

Finally, Claire goes limp. From her waif-like eyes, tears bubble out. She had seemed so arid, not only hollowed out like robins' bones, but as parched as a corn husk too. So her tears surprise me, like the first sign of potential biological life in Claire. The first indication of her humanity, the hundred-and-first indication of her anguish.

Claire's perfect face collapses into sobs. She rolls over, hiding her head in her arms, her body shaking from grief. I rub slow circles on her back.

"Mama?" It's Gracie in her nightgown in the doorway, her arms corralling a crowd of stuffed animals the way Claire's once did. "What's wrong?" The seal, the horse, the rabbit, the dog, and lion stare at me with button eyes.

"Nightmares," I say.

Gracie chooses the stuffed dog from among her brood and tucks it under one of Claire's arms. Then she disappears back to her fort.

I pat Claire. Her vertebrae feel like a porcelain necklace down her trembling back. A movement in the corner of my eye startles me. It is Dr. Ingram, lurching against the door-post. He puts a hand out and braces against the sideboard.

"Is everything all right?" he asks woozily.

Consciousness looks very dicey on him. I take a nanosecond auditory reading of the hurricane. Maybe if I call 911 again, an ambulance would be available to collect him in a few hours.

"Fine," I say. "Great."

Ingram feels Daddy's pulse with the backs of his fingers.

He says, "Maybe tonight isn't the time to resolve…" He makes a circular gesture with his hand.

I hold Claire until her stormy sobs dribble into whimpers and then into the long deep breaths that I take for sleep, and I keep my arm there because, well, I don't trust her.

Four of us in a scrum on the dining room floor. Like a melted heap of Madame Tussaud's wax figures. In my household, people do well to sleep with one eye open.

31

When I'm at least 18 percent sure Claire is asleep, I tiptoe to the kitchen. Ingram staggers into the darkness behind me. He makes a beeline for the back door and retrieves his raincoat.

"Miss Calaway, I brought a copy of your father's file with me."

He pulls a damp sheaf of paper from his inside coat pocket and sets it out on the kitchen table.

"I don't know what all this means," I say. There are columns galore, scribbly hieroglyphic records of physicians along the route. There are medications and doses that go back years.

"Psychotic disorders of all kinds turn up in midlife. We don't know why. After your father's assault, he was institutionalized for three months."

I need to organize myself. I am Jeffers Creskie, sailing down, down, into the sago palm. All sorts of strange memories are floating down onto my cheeks like soft, cold snowflakes. Something big is about to end for me.

"Your mother refused to press charges. This put the state in a peculiar position. How could they release a child molester back into the family? They tried to reason with your mother, but she wouldn't hear of it. She took him back. Of course, by now he was heavily medicated. But it allowed her the semblance of normalcy. Very few people knew what he'd done."

Ingram regards me with that pernicious brand of sympathy that makes single mothers cry. But I am curiously calm. I've been waiting for this news all my life. Some reluctant nerve bundle in my brain did the math and kept a seat warmed and waiting.

"Claire became pregnant from the rape. Your mother brought her to an unlicensed physician for an abortion. Claire hemorrhaged, and your mother was forced to bring her to the hospital."

"My mother tried to kill herself. The overdose."

"She gave Claire an overdose of painkillers. Probably an accident. They both went in the ambulance to the hospital."

"My mother. Was a monster."

"This was another era," says Ingram.

"Everyone makes excuses for her."

Ingram shrugs. "There is such a thing as poverty of the mind."

"She was inhumane."

A gust of wind slams the house with a cosmic *whomp*. The walls shudder.

Claire appears in the doorway. I don't know what she's overheard.

"There's somebody outside," she says.

I squint at the back door, and through the kitchen windows, but see nothing. "I'm sure it's—" I say.

"I saw someone."

"No one could be out in this."

Claire shoots me a pitying glance. She knows too well the limits of my imagination. "And yet there is, *en fait*. Anybody you know likes to visit during hurricanes?"

I gasp. I desperately scan the yard, but I see nothing.

"Miss Calaway," says Ingram. "I have your father's file here. I wonder if it might help you to see it."

"Help me?" Claire says bitterly. Her voice only just above the storm. Her pain and indignation palpable. "Did I forget something?"

"No, no," Ingram says. "You had asked me about medications. He was on extremely high doses of antipsychotics. We would never prescribe those levels today."

She is silent for a moment, drawing up a statement from the doorway. She looks like a soul prepared to detonate.

"Does it say in the file that he shit all over my sheets when he was done?" she asks.

"It mentions the abortion," Ingram says.

Claire whips her eyes to me. Secret one. Betrayed. She backs up against the wall, nearly cowering. She is as shaken now as the day it happened. It's too intimate. Too wrong. Too damaging. I move toward her, but she throws up two hands to stop me.

Claire points at the file. Even in the darkness, I can see the flicker of distress in her eyes.

"Does it mention the priest?" she asks.

"Priest?" I say.

"After the abortion. Mother took me to a priest to be exorcised."

Ingram drops soundlessly into a chair.

"Claire, I cannot. Cannot imagine." I can't move.

"Mother sat in the little vestibule the whole time," Claire says. "At this church way out on Katy Road. So no one would know. Don't you see? Even now, in total blackness, I can see your revulsion."

"No, Claire. Only horror on your behalf. Never revulsion."

"Did you ever seek help?" Ingram asks.

"From?" Claire cries out. "From adults?"

Why did help not descend upon this family? How deep was the South? Why did Social Services not take our parents away?

Claire sighs profoundly. "All that. Is that in your files?"

Now she's told. Now the secret is over. She slumps against the counter. She allows me to hold her in my arms.

"All those years," I say. "You looked at me over your cereal bowl and said nothing."

"I thought you'd hate me," Claire says. "For destroying what was left. What I'd give for a cup of coffee." She is drained and spent. She scans the countertop. "May I take an orange?"

"Anything," I say.

She takes one from the bowl. Slowly she peels it, the brilliant scent bursting into the room, trying to remind us of any good in life. A surge of wind batters the house with debris. Claire takes a few segments, eighteen or so calories' worth, and drifts back to the dining room where her rapist lies oblivious, having sipped the waters of Lethe years ago.

"I need to lie down," Ingram says. "I am terribly sorry, Miss Calaway. For all of it." He sways off to the living room.

The wind kicks up. Something hard clatters against an upstairs wall.

Later Claire comes to find me in the living room. Even in the dark, her pallor is stark. "I need a shower."

"It's going to be cold," I say.

"Gracie informed me."

I worry that the cold water will burn off the last rogue calorie that keeps Claire upright. "You should get some sleep," I say, burping up some vestige of normalcy.

"Okey dokey," she says, some of the Meatpacking District coming back into her voice. She drifts upstairs to the guest room. Who is she, now that the mystery is gone?

Gracie, queen of our battery-dependent airwaves, shouts groggily from her fort that Che is moving out at twenty-one miles per hour. "Surfside got hammered," she adds.

Ill-fated Surfside. Houston's airbag.

"Is no one asleep?" I say.

"It's too noisy," Gracie shouts.

Out the french doors water glistens. This could well be a house in the Louisiana bayou, sitting on stilts in a forsaken marsh. No one seems surprised when incest takes place in backwater swamps. No one blinks about pedophiles calling themselves preachers.

Gracie calls out that Kemah has recorded twelve inches of rain in the past hour. Information is power.

In that instant, I do see something moving outside the

windows. It snaps my mind out of its coma. I put my nose to the glass. The rain falls horizontally. Brutishly. It's hard to make anything out among the shrubs, the toppled palm. Huge oak and hackberry limbs have been pitched into the earth like knives. Ripped palm fronds flap on the ground until the wind picks them up again and carries them away. Someone's porch rocking chair is upside down in our turf, its finials stuck in the St. Augustine. A chill works its way up my spine.

"Gracie," I say, sticking my head near the fort entrance. "Why don't we give the batteries a rest and try to close our eyes."

"Okey dokey," she says, mimicking Claire.

"Big Ears."

I turn on my cell phone, which shows just a sliver of green juice, and call Lisa.

"Are you all right?" she asks groggily. "It's two in the morning there?"

"I—" I begin to cry.

"Julia."

"Oh, Lisa."

I tell her. A very short version. She's weeping by the end.

"I'm packing, Julia. I'll be there when the first plane lands."

"No, no. Fix your situation, Lisa. Put Hadges in a cage. Right something in Sodom."

"Poor Claire," she says, over and over. "Where is she now?"

"She went upstairs to rest."

My phone beeps.

"My cell phone is finished," I say. "I have to go charge it in the car."

Suddenly I hear a scrape of iron outside and twitch. I look out the back door window, trying to compose myself, fully aware that people's mailboxes are often airborne during these storms. I can't see a thing.

"Lisa," I say. "Something is wrong."

"Julia, everything is wrong right now."

Dark rainwater trickles under the kitchen door. It frightens me, the way it seeps slowly, almost thickly, like blood.

32

The rain drives in from the north, at an angle too low for doors and windows to prevent it. The noise is deafening. I return to the dining room and check Daddy's skin temperature for any sign that Claire veni-vidi-vici-ed and disappeared.

"It's louder than ever," Gracie shouts to me. I didn't even hear her come into the dining room. Her voice sounds different to me. "What's a girl got to do to get food around here?"

There's a loud crack outside, and I squint through gray water but see nothing.

"Mom," Gracie cries out. "I. Am. Hungry."

We walk into the kitchen. I cut up an apple for her. I'm just getting a glass of water when we hear the distinct scrape of wood against the house.

"What was that?" Gracie asks. She stops chewing.

"Probably a tree limb."

Then comes an unmistakable bang of iron.

Gracie whimpers. "Is somebody trying to get in our house?"

"Of course not, Gracie. Nobody's out in a hurricane. That's just someone's mailbox."

She pushes away from the table. "I'm not hungry anymore." She stares anxiously out the window.

"Hurricanes are full of scary noises." Does she hear the fright in my voice?

"No, something is wrong."

"Everything's fine," I say. And that's when the whole house shudders. We hear something smash explosively against the french doors of the dining room. There's a splintering of glass, a suck of air, a rush of storm sounds. A clang of metal. Instantly I smell the sea air. Instantly we feel the storm surge into our protected space.

"Mama?" Gracie mewls.

"Stay here, Gracie," I whisper, finger to my lips. "No, here." I stow her in the laundry closet. My heart beats wildly. Silently I lift my mother's heavy iron off the shelf and hold the handle with two hands the way it was never intended to be held. I steal toward the dining room. The air is wet and warm. The storm is inside now, bone-rattling. I hold the iron like a baseball bat.

"Hello?" I can't even hear myself. Wind is screaming into the house. Roy's crap lumber floor vibrates with footsteps. I lunge toward the dining room. Framed by shards of french doors is the figure of an intruder in a rain-slick poncho. Water and debris fly in behind him. He has Daddy's old iron shovel clenched brutishly in his hands, and he's swept a path with it. Chairs are toppled and what's left of the modest chandelier is swinging by wires.

And I see it. I see it in his form. In his gestures. It is Bobby.

"No!" I scream. "You animal!"

Bobby advances on me with his shovel held high. I tighten my grip on the iron. He readies for a swing, and I see the wide arc of iron swirling toward my head. Automatically, I duck and my arms go up and I feel the sickening thud of heavy metal against my shoulder. The pain feels like fire. It flashes through my whole arm and I sink to the floor with a cry.

But that's not enough. Not anymore. Adrenalin lifts me. I see Bobby recover from his swing. The shovel is heavy and awkward and takes some effort to regain. In that moment I leap at Bobby, set my feet square on the crap wood floor and swing the iron at his head with all my might—all my might and rage.

I swing, and I hit. Just like all those backyard baseball

games, when the Berry boys underestimated the Calaway girls and gave us soft pitches. The old iron connects with Bobby's head for a horrible crunch, and I hear his groan through the storm's howling. He sinks to the floor, dropping the shovel with a clang.

This time it's me pulling back my weapon for a second blow. But Bobby grabs my ankle and I tumble backward onto the floor, the iron's weight toppling me off balance. My head hits with a thump, and I am weirdly aware that real fighting is not like in the movies. Real violence is mud ugly.

A curtain of black shimmers in front of my eyes. I blink, trying to wash it away. Bobby slowly, determinedly rises up beside me. I hear the scrape of the old shovel up and off the floor. I can't think. My legs won't work. I try to roll to the side, but I bump into Daddy's mattress. Desperately, I roll to the other side. Bobby roars. I cover my head with my arms. And that's when I hear a deafening *CRACK!*

The shape that is Bobby staggers and falls backward through the glass, splashing onto the soaked lawn. The shovel tumbles with a thud onto Daddy, then bounces to the floor.

Claire stands in the doorway, legs akimbo. My gun in her outstretched arms.

Slowly she lowers the gun and comes to me. She sinks to the floor. I hold her thin trembling form in my arms. She's speaking, but I can't hear anything over the storm.

Dr. Ingram lists into the doorway of the dining room and takes in the scene. He lowers himself to the floor carefully and puts two fingers on Daddy's throat. He closes Daddy's eyes.

I hug Claire, rocking her as I might a baby, whispering uselessly into the roar of the storm. I need to get Gracie.

Ingram puts his mouth to my ear. "We can't move the bodies," he yells. "Until the police arrive. No, please don't be alarmed. This was self-defense. Please, Julia, trust me."

Claire mumbles incoherently. Her body twitches. We draw

her into the hallway and I close the dining room door, realizing this is the first time I've ever shut that door, and wishing
something magical would seal it forever and make the dining
room vanish from the house.

I race to collect Gracie, who has been shivering in the
laundry room, and we all gather in the living room in a state
of numbness. Ingram drapes a blanket over Claire's shaking
skeleton. I wrap Gracie in a fleece blanket and pull her onto
my lap.

"Who was it?" Gracie asks.

"A stranger," says Ingram.

"Is it over?"

"All over," he says.

"What happened to Claire?" Gracie pursues.

"Claire was very brave," I say.

"Take some slow breaths," Ingram cautions Claire. He
turns to me. "Do you have any Xanax or Valium in your
bathroom cabinet?"

I nod and take Gracie with me. I can just hear the doctor
flick open his cell phone and call in an emergency. I'm not
sure what Gracie should or shouldn't know. Sweet Jesus. Is
this what my mother wondered? What to tell the little girl?

We stop in the kitchen to collect some water, wine, and
crackers. This was the way the hurricane was supposed to
be—strange picnics in unusual places at ridiculous hours of
the morning. A sense of the abnormal tinged with mischief,
not terror.

"The hurricane," Gracie says. "It's leaving."

I pause to listen. "You're right."

Ingram coaxes a few sips of wine and two pills into Claire.

Gracie is on my lap and we both have an arm on Aunt
Claire.

"Is it over?" Gracie asks.

"Yes," Ingram says. He's become the acting captain of
this ship.

"Why would someone want to break in?" Gracie says.

"To get out of the storm."

Ingram glances at me. "EMS will be here as soon as they can. I expect it will be several hours. I wonder if we could close our collective eyes in the meantime."

He arranges Claire's limbs on the couch. She's strangely obedient. Then he lowers himself into an armchair across from her. Gracie pulls me into her fort.

"We're safe in here," she says. "Right?"

"Totally."

"It's all over."

"Entirely."

"Do you want one of my pillows, Mama?"

"That would be great. Thank you."

"I don't know if I can get to sleep. Don't leave me, Mama."

"Never."

And that's the last sound I hear from her. I fall asleep slowly and awkwardly—my brain a sputtering jalopy that jerks, backfires, and finally stalls.

That wasn't so bad. What was bad was waking up.

At first light, we're jolted awake to the siren song of Gracie screaming, "Roach!" with such intensity I feel defibrillated.

One poor bastard has crept in for sanctuary, but he wasn't going to be the ultimate survivor of his race. *Crunch*, he says, under my shoe.

I cock my head. It's pure silence outside. "Listen, Gracie. It's over."

The hurricane is gone. Our street is under water. I wipe the dead roach from my shoe and put my nose to the front door glass, and peer at the carnage outside.

"Good morning."

Ingram's voice startles me. Gracie's roach alarm must have roused him. He doesn't look the better for a few hours of sleep. His stitches—my stitches—are ghastly. His skin is the color of skimmed milk with an expired sell-by date. "It's over then," the doctor says. He's struck by the peculiar brand of hush.

I show him the world outside, which is now a bayou, with fallen trees half-in, half-out of the water, whole branches dangling like Spanish moss, and sludge lapping at my front stoop. We open the door and smell the cool air. There is no discernible noise. Only the toads are out, making small reluctant leaps across the debris. An old oak on the Berrys' front lawn snapped about thirty feet up, and the top half has fallen onto something.

"My car," Ingram says. It's a Range Rover, with a tree through the roof.

"I can still heat water," I say. "Would you like a cup of tea?"

He follows me to the kitchen. Passing the bar he pauses.

"Is that my blood?" He points to the peonies in scab-black on the wall.

"Claire is an artist."

In the kitchen, we find Gracie dunking a banana into a dish of granola. "Is the roach gone?" she asks. On the table beside her is a flyswatter.

"No more hurricanes for him," I say.

"Is the stranger gone?" she asks.

"All taken care of," Ingram says. "That is entirely over."

Gracie nods. She glances down at her dish. "Mama, I cannot look at granola one more day."

"Gracie, it's been less than twelve hours."

"Let's evacuate."

Ingram sips hot black tea. Dots of healthy pink collect across his skin.

"I'm going to stay with you until the emergency services arrive," he says. "Then I should return to the hospice. I imagine I'm needed there."

Ingram is a need-o-holic. I say, "Shouldn't you go to the

hospital and get stitched properly, and maybe get a little more blood, and maybe also a tetanus shot?"

Gracie leans toward Dr. Ingram and shakes her head. "She's always like this."

I laugh. With mythic relief. I'm so glad I look the same to her.

EPILOGUE

Daddy died this morning at around three-thirty a.m., a result of old age and a crushing blow to his forehead from an iron shovel, his old iron shovel, which once planted a Phoenix palm and moved stone dust under our front stoop. It was high time for Daddy to head to his lower eighty-five.

Hurricane Che left a cool front in its wake. I opened the doors and windows to let the house breathe. The police and ambulances arrived toward noon, having sent emergency personnel ahead to unclog street drains dammed by felted leaves and dead possum. We watched them from the living room, and it seemed like a small miracle each time hints of curbs and lawns appeared. Promptly after that, an affecting little parade of vehicles with flashing lights drove through the low water and stopped in front of our house. Only at that moment did I realize I'd felt marooned here, at the end of an abandoned cul-de-sac, in a city devastated by a hurricane, which wasn't supposed to be so terrible.

We all sat on the sofa, Gracie on my lap, Ingram on my right, and Claire on my left. Claire was on a nice cloud of booze and tranquilizer heaven, but she blinked if I nudged her. A kind-faced policeman introduced himself as Sergeant Pineda. He looked like he'd been up all night, too. He settled across the coffee table in a chair too small for his bulk. The saddle leather of his gun belt creaked when he readjusted. I could just imagine his wife swatting at his big swollen hands when he reached for another wedge of pecan pie.

Our story had confused him. "It wasn't your gun?" the policeman asked Claire.

"No," I said.

"*Nyet*," Gracie whispered, her angel's voice disembodied

by exhaustion and sedatives from Ingram's car.

"It was mine," I said. "I'd forgotten about it."

The policeman looked up. Nodded. "I see." He made a mark on his paperwork. "That was quite a shot, miss," he added to Claire, who was immune to verbal interactions. It was clear Officer Pineda didn't know whether to pat poor Claire on her bony shoulder or lock her up. We didn't look too threatening—any of us. We looked like we'd just been through a hurricane, spit out into this living room like grit from Corpus Christi. Ingram had medicated us into submissive eunuchs after I told Gracie about her father.

"Let me get this straight," the policeman said. "The gun was in the guest room. Your sister was staying in there. She saw an intruder and got the gun and shot him. Did you—" he looked at Claire. "Did you know the intruder?"

"No," Claire said.

Gracie made a small noise.

I said, "With the doors broken open, the whole storm was whipping into the room. We could hardly see."

"It was your husband, wasn't it?"

"My ex. And she only met him once, twelve years ago."

Sergeant Pineda lifted his eyebrows. "Pardon my French, but this is a helluva thing. And, Doc, you look like the walking dead."

Ingram took the opportunity to put his hand briefly on my knee. "Is that sedative kicking in for you?"

"I still have a little sensation in my left thumb," I said.

"Mama," Gracie moaned, tears leaking from her eyes.

I engulfed Gracie in my arms and whispered those phrases of absolute love. Her skin was warm under layers of fleece. Outside was inside. The front door was gaping open while a pageant of policemen and medical personnel plodded in and out. The dining room was cleaved open to the elements, and while the rain had stopped, twenty-two inches of water were now trying desperately to evaporate.

"So, Doc," the policeman said kindly. "That gash of yours

wasn't related to the accident?"

"No."

The officer nodded. "I think we're wrapped up here. With all due respect, Doc, I wouldn't go back to that plastic surgeon."

Claire broke her code of unconsciousness and let out a concise human laugh.

Ingram gave me a kind, reassuring glance.

A police officer with a clipboard full of forms leaned over to speak with Pineda. She had a silver cross necklace on, and it swung in the air when she bent over. "Do we classify the second death as storm-related?" she asked.

The big officer shrugged. "What the hell."

Ingram said, "If you're done then? This family needs rest."

"Do you all have a place to go?" the policeman asked. "Someplace where we can reach you if we need to?"

From my left came the low and lilty voice of Claire, whose arms were once jammed with stuffed puppies and euphoric hopes and no idea whatsoever that people could kill the intangible things.

"We'll be at the Hotel Derek," she said.

We only learned later, as the facts dribbled out, how badly damaged the city was. Four and a half million people without power. Central power lines toppled, Galveston uninhabitable, no water, no food, no ice. Houston had that Biblical disaster look. A seventy-day flood, in the final analysis, could hardly have done a better job.

The city looked like a lump of Brazos River clay. Thousands of trees lay tangled in their own branches. Sidewalks flipped up. A film of leaves and dirt and petroleum-sodden silt covered the city, making neighborhoods impassable and toxic. Trash was stuck everywhere—fast-food drink cups, plastic bags, paper, bits of clothing, cardboard. The famous Humble landfill had annexed Houston.

Hurricane Che sucked in a cool front, worth a mention to blessing-counters. In the cloudless blue sky, massive black helicopters buzzed to the Ship Channel and back down to League City and back up to the inner loop. The governor flew over to survey the damage. The media were calling Che one of the worst storms of the century.

Under several quilts on the tenth floor of the Hotel Derek (which had backup generators), Claire and I passed on the media coverage and clicked to the movie channel, where Cary Grant was flashing his rakish smile on a huge flat-panel TV. Our mother may have said no to Cary Grant, but at least five other women said yes, and one was cavorting with him on the Riviera in black and white. In the movie at least, he didn't seem to be aware of his loss.

Claire and I made a sandwich of Gracie on Claire's king-sized bed. We were spoiled on room service and Claire's penchant for good champagne, which Dr. Ingram assured me was therapeutic for dealing with shock. He added, as an aside, that Claire's food issues might require a different type of therapy. At some point later. Much later.

I couldn't ask Claire, the furtive sniper, if she'd meant to kill the intruder, if she'd known it was Bobby. I'd have said it was a lucky shot if I hadn't seen her stance, which indicated serious firearms training.

"How did you find that gun?" I asked.

"I was snooping," she shrugged. Ever since, she'd been like the coyote that ate the chicken; not another word, lest a feather got burped up by mistake.

My house was wrapped in yellow crime scene tape. I could just imagine Mimi Blanton's horrified face when she fluttered back into town. I didn't want that old house anymore. The childhood memories were bad enough, but the new ones were worse. Claire took photographs of all my drawings in the attic. Together, in her Derek suite, we emailed them to New York, to Pitti Palazzo, which gave not a damn for hurricanes or funerals. I would whitewash those walls and pack up my supplies and let someone else try to plant zinnias in that front yard. Gracie and I were moving.

Claire grew up thinking she was the victim of a family crime; but she was the victim of several. We Calaways testified to the supreme limitations of human nature. I won't let the same thing happen to Gracie—none of us will. On the way to the Hotel Derek, Gracie turned her tear-stained face to Claire and wailed about her father, and Claire said, "Well, you've got me now."

Gracie paused mid-wail and looked at me in bewilderment. "Is that a good thing?"

Claire rolled her eyes and laughed like a rusty hinge and promised, "I'm going to get nicer, Gracie, just for you."

I closed my eyes with the pure, bone-deep contentment of hearing Claire's voice. That's when Hussar and his stretch limousine pulled into the Derek's entrance. He said something to me in scoldy Arabic, and I warned him not to eat the fish from our front lawn (I'd seen him slip one into his trunk), and then I carried Gracie upstairs to Claire's ridiculously large suite. We were treated like kings by the hotel staff, because we were among the handful that intended to pay our bill.

Gracie was asleep by the time Cary Grant got his girl, and she didn't wake up when the phone on the bedside table rang.

"It's me," Lisa's voice sang out.

"We're okay," I said. Drunk. Banged up. Medicated into Zen states.

"I know."

"We're at the Derek."

"I know."

"Well, what don't you know?"

"What suite number. I'm downstairs in the lobby."

I choked on a bolus of champagne.

"Don't be a blonde," Lisa snorted.

"Send her up," Claire said.

We ordered hot coffee and ate fresh migas while Houston began digging out of the wreckage.

"You both don't seem exactly devastated," Lisa observed. "Or maybe it's just the champagne."

She was right there in front of me on the bed, cute short bangs and brown hair with $650 Sally Hershberger highlights in real life. And Claire. The last time we were all together was at my wedding, when Claire came late, smoked, left.

"You all look awful," Lisa said. "Except Gracie, who's perfect." She stroked Gracie's sleeping form.

Gracie, my everything, would have the toughest row to hoe. As I tucked her into the vast hotel bed, I promised to be there with her, and she in turn promised to help me with my hottest new project—a new clothing line called Pitti Petite, for little girls with fashion mojo.

Lisa, all wonderful nose and brown bangs, was by my feet. Claire, all bones and orange spikes, was on my right. I was taking in the infusions of heaven. Whatever our mother took from us, she left us each other.

"What's going on with your job?" I asked Lisa.

"Recant-aroni," she replied. "Hadges makes a lousy con. The paperwork had a million flaws."

"So back to work?"

"Yes. Maybe. I don't know. It's a little like falling out of love. Once the scales drop from your eyes…" Lisa's gaze drifted down toward the floor. The skin around her eyes was rippled with fatigue. "I need to wash my face. Will you design me a beautiful dress, Julia? Aging is hell. I think it's time to do that-which-must-not-be-named in the dark."

Claire laughed. Lisa grinned. She gave me a swift strangling hug and disappeared to the bathroom. Claire's suite had about five of them, all appointed with French-milled everything.

I turned to Claire. "I must have been a house plant not to know what happened. And you've been carrying around this wreckage for so long all by yourself."

"No more love," she said, the corners of her mouth curling into a baffling dimple. "Or I won't be able to paint anymore."

She wandered off into another compartment of her suite. Claire reminded me of the kind of people that inhabit dreams. They turn up and they vanish. They say oblique things that mean too much and leave you to parse it out. They roam alien beaches or sit on desolate chairs in rooms with slanting plank floors. These were geographies of the imagination, and Claire lived there. I used to find her when I slept—Claire, for whom I mourned, and those that strangled her. A part of me has been sleeping all my life.

Out of the hotel window I surveyed the wreckage of Che. Nothing moved. Signs and awnings hung shredded, no breeze to ripple them. Trees were toppled into lumps of debris. Westheimer lay under a film of trash and mud. The sky was ash grey, and the earth looked like a cosmic plumbing disaster.

But underneath was life. And I would be able to live it now. I had learned the dire secrets that kept me in a tidy box, and now I could dissolve the limits of my ability to be more.